Naughty Nights

Kate White

pencil

ISBN 978-93-5610-648-2
© Kate White 2022
Published in India 2022 by Pencil

A brand of
One Point Six Technologies Pvt. Ltd.
123, Building J2, Shram Seva Premises,
Wadala Truck Terminal, Wadala (E)
Mumbai 400037, Maharashtra, INDIA
E connect@thepencilapp.com
W www.thepencilapp.com

Author biography

Kate White was born and raised in the beautiful country, Bulgaria, among nature and lovely and playful pets. Kate considers her freedom, independence, and self-improvement to be most important to her. If she isn't spending time being completely obsessed with her projects, you can almost always find her on the road or with a book in hand.

CONTENTS

Chapter 1

"It's so cold!" I whisper getting out of the cabin in Sweden, Jokkmokk, thinking about the warm climate in Honolulu. But I wanted some snow. Especially when Christmas is coming. I smile and move my gaze to the landscape in front of me. All forest! Except for the cabin one kilometer from here. It's so peaceful and quiet. I must enjoy it to the fullest while I can because my family is coming tomorrow night.

I go through the forest and the snow. I see a male figure going after a moose. And here's where the shoot came from. I hear another shot. I focus on the moose who fell almost immediately after the shot and I go to it. I start examing the animal's legs when someone shouts. "I'm sorry but I shot it." I look carefully at the moose and then I look up.

Tall, about 180 centimeters, and obviously fit, even though the layers of clothes on, man is standing up in front of me. He has styled black hair, mischievous brown, almost black eyes, and a slight smile. Where have I seen him before? "Take it. I will catch another one." He says actually commanding me. "It is not needed. I buy animal products from farms."

He looks at me up and down. "Is it you who live up there?" He asks with his calm, deep voice and I nod. "Jonathan Edmeades." He introduces himself taking and kissing my hand. "Karolina Fedorova," I reply. "I am going now. Have a nice day, Mr. Edmeades." I wave and head back to the cabin.

When I get into the kitchen, my phone vibrates. It is a message from my mother telling me the flight is canceled and they are coming the day after tomorrow. I text her back saying it's okay and start making myself lunch. Taking the products out of the fridge, I notice I don't have some for the meal. I grab my keys and get in the car.

I am in the grocery store looking for turmeric when I hear a male voice. "Mrs. Fedorova, it is a pleasure to see you again." He says with his eyes on me and a little smile creeping on his face. "It is a pleasure to see you, too, Mr. Edmeades," I say and finally find what I was searching for. "Preparing for lunch?" I nod. "Yes, I am. And in the process, I understood I was out of some... stuff." I answer while grabbing some avocados. "Are you in a hurry?" He asks me. "Not exactly. Why?"

"I would like to have coffee with you." He says sounding bossy not actually asking. At that moment I see something in his eyes. I can't explain what but I see it but it kinda scares me and at the same time pulls me towards him. "Okay. Just after shopping. Is that okay?" I ask. Universe, forgive me, please! "Of course, Mrs. Fedorova. And I have to buy some things, too." He answers and I see it again. I bite my lip. "Okay," I say nodding, every single muscle tensed in my body and my breath on hold. I turn and walk away releasing my breath. I grab one last thing, batteries, pay and go out.

I take a very deep breath and exhale slowly through my mouth. I put the bags on the back seats and then I see Mr. Edmeades doing the same. He comes to me and takes my hand. "Shall we?" I swallow hard unknowingly why and nod.

We enter a fancy cafe, called cafe Gasskas. It is almost like a house, a yellow two-floor one and there are no many people. Mr. Edmeades chooses a table near the window and we sit. "What brings you here, Mrs. Fedorova?" He asks and I bring my attention from outside the window to him. "I like snow at Christmas. And since in Honolulu there's no such a thing as snow, I chose to come here. I can learn and have an amazing Christmas at the same time." I answer with a little smile on my face and order green tea with lemon. Mr. Edmeades orders black coffee and the waitress goes away. "What about you, Mr. Edmeades?"

"Just Jonathan, please. Well, it looks like we are here because of the same reasons. And it is surprising to me that I haven't seen you before. Since we both live in Honolulu. It may be because I travel a lot recently." He says and looks at me as if digging into my soul. I swallow hard. A waiter brings our drinks and I almost immediately sip of it. The tea was hot but it calmed me down. "Are you okay, Karolina? You seem tensed up."

"I am fine." I hurry with an answer. Jonathan purses his lips and tilts his head to his right a little. I bite my lip and look away. Why am I so nervous? I question myself looking at some children playing outside. "Do you love kids?" I hear Jonathan's voice. "I do. But I do not plan on having one soon." I answer still looking through the window. "Are you free tonight, Mrs. Fedorova?" He asks me which makes me turn face to face with him. "Depends on what you mean by 'tonight', Mr. Edmeades."

"Like 6 PM." He says and darkness crosses his eyes. I nod. "I do not have plans for 6 PM. For now." I say looking at my watch and then up at him. He tilts his head to his right again and a trace of a smirk appears on his face. I bite my lip and release my breath I didn't know I was holding. "Okay, then," Jonathan says and then asks for the check.

Chapter 2

I hit play on Whethan and Dua Lipa's High and close my eyes feeling the rhythm. I start moving, touching my body and radiating confidence and sexiness.

The song is about to end when bangs on the front door pull me away from my trance and I jump a little. I turn around and see Jonathan standing next to the door wearing a grey formal suit. I freeze. "There is half an hour to six!" I say waiting for an explanation. "I know. But I brought you something I want you to wear." He says and my breath hitches. He gives me a small box and I take it. "Open it!" He says and I am about to do so when High starts over again. I look up with my eyes wide and rush to stop it but Jonathan's hand stops me. "No need. I like the song. Go, get dressed." I nod and climb the stairs and head to my bedroom. I close the door and get undressed listening to the music coming down the stairs. I put on black jeans and a blouse, a brown coat, and boots. I look in the mirror.

My long dark brown hair falling on my shoulders fits perfectly with my hazel eyes and my almost pale complexion. I am here for two weeks and my so-called tan is already gone. I look at my outfit and thank myself for the workouts, being active and eating the right food. I notice the small box Jonathan gave me. I take it and open it carefully.

A necklace with a heart-shaped diamond. I put it back.

I go down the stairs and The Chain plays on. "You have an intriguing taste in music." Jonathan points out and looks up from my laptop. He looks me up and down. "Where are we going?"I ask interrupting his checking out. "Why are you not wearing it?" I look at the beautiful black box in my hands and hand it to him. "I can not wear it. This is a real diamond." He takes the box from my hands, opens it and takes the necklace in his hands. He comes behind me and moves my hair aside. "I brought it for you to wear it." He says near my ear sending shivers down my spine. He places it on my neck and then turns me around to face him. I bite my lip. He comes closer.

I step back and take a deep breath. "We should probably go... wherever that is..." I say and stop the music. I look at Jonathan and before someone of us says something our phones beep. I grab mine and see the news. An awful snowstorm?! Are you kidding me?! "I hope you are prepared," Jonathan says and reading the next sentences I realized what he meant. The meteorologists say that it is best if everyone stays indoors for the next 32 hours, counting from now.

"Preparation is not a problem. I have everything I need. You are the one you have a problem." I say and sit down on the couch. "And what exactly is my problem?" He asks and sits across from me. "You can't leave. And your bodyguard is outside." I say but opposite of the reaction I expect he smiles. "Karolina, could you please look through the window?" I look at him and slowly stand up. I go to the window and see the bodyguard is missing. "I send him a message to leave the second I got the news. And about leaving... that is not my problem." He smirks. "Mine neither," I say and smile. "I am going to change into something comfortable."

I pick an over-sized pullover with a triangle neckline, jeggings, and knitted socks. I go downstairs and see Jonathan is lying on the sofa comfortably with his jacket and shoes taken off. "I see you made yourself comfortable." I pause for a moment. "Are you up for dinner?" I ask. "Only if I help." He answers and stands up. I nod and we enter the kitchen.

"Where is the flour?" Jonathan asks me. "The middle cupboard," I answer quickly. He opens it but I notice he doesn't make any other move. "What is it?" I ask chopping a green paper. He looks at me. "You don't have flour." I leave the knife and stand by Jonathan's side. "Here it is," I say standing on my tiptoes reaching for the coconut flour. I give it to him with a smile. "See the word flour?" I place my finger below the word. "That was not what I was searching for." He answers and I return to chopping. "You won't find that kind of flour in my house. Or any food containing gluten... or milk." He looks at me. "I have celiac disease," I explain. "Oh! I didn't know. Sorry." I smile. "No need to apologize, Mr. Edmeades."

"When did you find out about the fact you have celiac disease?" He asks and puts the coconut flour aside turning towards me. "I was about 18 years old when I was diagnosed. But my symptoms... they had always been there.

The serious ones started appearing when I was in my teenage years. Bloating, constant abdominal pain, changes in weight, trouble with sleeping and falling asleep. Fatigue, anemia, headaches, bone pains, depression, anxiety, trembling hands and on and on. Then I developed lactose intolerance at the age of seventeen. And I was constantly needing help..." I stop for a second remembering some painful memories. "Why constant help? You just need a few tests."

"That's right. But when your mother is working all day long for bills, food, school... and at the same time is telling you 'It's just a new virus.' every single time you try to explain... well, you get the point." I put the fish with avocado and vegetables in the oven. I turn towards Jonathan and smile. "Tell me more about yourself. You mentioned depression." He says and I cross my arms. "I think it's enough tragedies for tonight," I say and see Balbina, my Russian blue cat. I grab her in my hands and hug her. "This is Balbina. And Charlie is upstairs. He is a golden retriever."

"A cat and a dog." He says, Balbina's eyes on him. "Yep. I love both cats and dogs and having them prove that opposites can make peace. And even love each other." I kiss Balbina's forehead and put her down. "Do the names mean something?" Jonathan asks. "Balbina means strong and powerful in Latin origin. Charlie means free man." I answer. "Why Russian blue and a retriever?" He asks me. "Are you really that curious?"

"You can understand a lot for a person just by the decisions they make. And something tells me you don't just choose something by a whim." He says and I smile. "Russian blues are sweet-tempered, loyal, social creatures who also enjoy alone time and are highly intelligent. Also, they don't shed much and produce lower levels of the glycoprotein Fel d 1, a known allergen, than other cat breeds. Golden Retrievers are kind, friendly, intelligent, confident and active."

"So I was right. And how did you choose the names?" I put my hands on my hips and I raise my eyebrow. "Isn't it obvious?" I answer him with a question and he smiles still waiting for the answer. I sigh. "To go through the hard moments in my life I had to be strong. And freedom is my priority. If I have freedom, I have everything."

Chapter 3

It is just after dinner and I am cleaning around when I see Jonathan coming to me without a t-shirt. And I would lie if I say my hormones didn't react. "Let me guess. You realized you don't bring clothes with you." I say putting the plates in the washing machine. "I sleep naked." He answers and I get his calmness now. "Okay," I say quietly and turn around feeling his smirk. "What is it then?" I ask. "Where should I sleep?" He answers my question with a question. I turn towards him. "Well, two bedrooms are prepared for my family's arrival and the one across mine is free, so feel free to use it."

"Okay. Is there anything you need help with?" He asks and I shake my head in response. "You can go." I grab my laptop and headphones and sit down on the sofa with my legs crossed. I open the laptop, play 'On' by BTS, and start writing down ideas for the book I am working on. Just then Jonathan comes to the sofa, takes my headphones, and sits next to me. Here comes the question. "Are you avoiding me?" I stop the music and close my laptop. "I just got some ideas I wanted to write down. But, yeah. Just a little." I answer honestly. "Why, am I bothering you?" He asks with a smirk on his face. I put my laptop away and stand up, biting my lips. "I am going to my room." And just then my phone starts ringing. "Здравствуйте!" - Hello! - I say.

"Здравствуйте! Как дела?" - Hello! How are you? - I hear my father asking me. "Я в порядке. А как насчет вас и мальчиков?" - I'm fine. What about you and the boys?

"Мы в порядке. Есть ли у вас планы на предстоящее Рождество?" - We are fine. Do you have plans for the upcoming Christmas? - He asks me. "Моя мама приезжает с остальной семьей. Они останутся здесь на два дня. Почему?" - My mother is coming over with the rest of the family. They will be staying here for two days. Why? - I answer him wondering why he is asking me. "Я думал о том, чтобы провести некоторое время вместе во время каникул." - I was thinking about spending some time together during the holidays. - He says and surprises me. I wasn't expecting that.

"Вы можете приехать. Я хотел бы провести время с вами тремя." - You can come. I would love to spend time with the three of you. - I say with hope. "А как насчет других?" - What about the others? - He asks and I bite my lip nervously. "Я буду думать о чем-то. Но если это проблема, вы можете прийти, когда они уйдут. Тогда мы можем принять рейс в Гонолулу." - I will think of something. But if it's a problem, you can come when they leave. Then we can take the flight to Honolulu.

"Я думаю, что это лучший вариант." - I think this is a better option. - He says and I smile. "Ладно. У нас есть сделка." - Okay. We have a deal. - We hang up the phone and when my eyes go up I see Jonathan watching me. "What?" I ask. "I am just curious... who were you talking to?"

"My biological father," I answer and look at his face. "He was asking if I have plans for Christmas so we, he and the boys - my two half-brothers, can spend the holidays together. And since I already have plans, which include my mother, second father, brother, and sister, they can't come. The main reason is the risk of ruining the holidays." I answer as simply as I could and sit on the couch near me. "I couldn't understand. I am an only child."He sits across me.

"Well. Things are just more complicated and funny. Like the upcoming situation." I say and he looks at me. "What situation?" He asks. "When they intersect and have to stay in the same house for one night," I answer and get up. "Now I am going to my room. If you need anything, you know where to find me."

Chapter 4

I take off my pullover and see my reflection. I see the small bird tattoo on my right side of the chest, the roses tattoo on my right arm, the love yourself inscription on my inner left upper arm, and when I turn around I see the lotus flower tattoo on my back. I take off the rest of my clothes and put on my satin pajama made up of a t-shirt and shorts. I lift up my hair into a messy bun, turn on the red light, so it is easier for me to fall asleep, and go to the bathroom to brush my teeth. I hear a knock on my door and the next second it opens. "I don't remember saying 'come in'." I enter the bathroom. "What is it anyway?" I ask and start brushing my teeth. "I was bored. Nice atmosphere!" He answers and lays down on my bed. I finish, enter my bedroom and put my hands on my hips. "What does that have to do with me?"

"You are the only person here and I thought we can talk." He explains and I soften my expression. "Okay." I sit on my bed crossed-leg and look at him. His medium-length black hair is a little messy, his perfect skin pleases you to touch it, his deep brown eyes are watching me. My look goes down and I notice his tattoos. On his right arm, there is a tattoo saying Not until we are lost do we begin to understand ourselves. On his chest are depicted wings of a devil, I suppose. Another tattoo, if not now then when is gently lying on the inside of his left wrist. "Like what you see?" He interrupts my gazing and I move my look away.

Suddenly Jonathan puts his head on my tighs and makes himself comfortable. I look at him in confusion. "I never thought you are the kind of person who has tattoos." He comments checking out the roses on my arm when he notices it. I just stay silent observing his actions. He gets up with a little frowned expression and looks at the bird and love yourself tattoos. "Is there more?" He asks and I nod. "One on the back." He gets up to see it and then comes back on his previous place examing the roses. He looks up at me and I swallow. "Relax." He mutters and I breathe out the air I didn't realize I was holding.

He comes closer so I can feel his hot breath on my skin and his upper lip touching my bottom lip. The blood in my veins is rushing, my heart pounding. Breathing heavily I close my eyes and then I feel his lips on mine. My whole being explodes with this one action and my hands make their way to his silky hair. Kissing me hungrily, Jonathan wraps his hand around my waist and lays me down. Moving his hand down to my thigh, he hovers over me placing himself between my legs and presses his body against mine. I moan when I feel his erection against my core. I wrap my legs around his waist and he moves his other hand to my shirt only to unbutton it and expose my breast. He cups the left one but then stands up. I look at him and see he is taking off his pants. I admire his perfectly fit body for a while.

I move a little, just so I can reach my pillow and take off my shirt. When Jonathan comes back over me naked, I wrap my legs around him again and find his tasty lips. He places his hands on my hips and tears up the fabric of my shorts and lacy underwear leaving me completely naked. Unknowingly why I smile a bit. He throws away the remains of my clothes. "Just a second." He whispers and reaches for his pants to take a condom. He tears the packet with his teeth and rolls the condom on his erected member.

Jonathan comes over me once again, kisses me and enters into me slowly. I let out a soft moan. "Fuck!" He groans and kisses me again. Moving in and out, he goes to my neck and places a kiss. Hands all over the bodies, heavy breathing, moans. All as if a dream. He speeds up and grabs my body. I turn us over so I can be on the top. I thrust in and bite my bottom lip. Jonathan grabs my hip with his right hand while his left is pulling me down to his lips.

He flips us and I am again on my back. He enters into me, a moan escapes my mouth and my back arches. His hand goes down to my clit making me see stars. "Jonathan..." I moan. He groans. My walls clench around his dick giving the best orgasm in my life and with one last thurst, he comes, too. He kisses me and lays down on my side, breathing heavily.

Jonathan grabs the blanket and wraps us up in it. He hugs me and I make myself comfortable. "So, is that the way you wanted to talk?" I ask with a slight smile on my face. "I really just wanted to talk with you. But the atmosphere, you in that outfit and all... Oh and I would say I'm sorry about your shorts and that irresistible lacy underwear... but I'm kinda not." I laugh. He looks at me with a smile and then kisses me.

Chapter 5

I wake up at 5 AM and Jonathan is sleeping next to me. I check my heart rate, get up, drink a glass of water and get into my workout clothes, high waist black leggings, and a long-sleeved black crop top. I brush my teeth, wash my face and do my hair in a ponytail. When I finish my workout, I prepare for my meditation. Candles, a mix of aromatherapy oils and a little statue of Buddha, because I practice Zen Buddhism. And about Christmas, I don't actually celebrate it, I just gather all the family members and spend time with them. I close my eyes and start chanting and concentrating on my breathing. After some time the bell rings and I take one final deep breath. I clean up and go to the bathroom for a cold shower. The cold water wakes me up fully.

I wrap myself up with a towel and get out of the bathroom. "Good morning!" Jonathan says and my eyes meet his. He is laying down, his hands behind his head, gazing at me with his mischievous eyes. "Good morning!" I reply to him and make my way to the closet. I grab the hairdryer and start drying out my hair. After a while, I feel arms wrapping up around me from behind. I look at the mirror and see Jonathan who is still naked, with messy hair and completely relaxed. I stop the hairdryer. "Come back to the bed with me." He whispers sending chills down to my spine. I turn around and just when I'm about to speak up, Jonathan kisses me. He removes the towel, throws it away and lifts me up. I wrap up my legs around his waist. "Jonathan..." I whisper-moan trying to think of something. I know I already slept with him the first day we met but half of me, probably the right one, is telling me that I shouldn't do that again.

Jonathan carries me to the bed and places me softly on the mattress. Then he comes to my side and wraps us with the blanket. I look at him with confusion. "Your body tensed up a lot." He explains. I grab the blanket and press it with a fist against my chest. "I have to get up!" I say and stand up. "You are avoiding me again." He sits up while saying it but I just go into the closet. I pick black lingerie, black jeans, and a green V-neck sweater. "We met yesterday. And I already slept with you!" I put on the lingerie and grab the jeans. "I don't think you had something against it yesterday," Jonathan says coming in the closet with his boxers and pants on. 'Yeah, I didn't have anything against it and I know why.'

"You are right, I didn't. And I know why." I start putting the jeans on. "Because you look hot and when you fucking kissed me, my hormones exploded... Along with my mind apparently." I stand up tall and see Jonathan coming to me. The next second I'm on my makeup table, Jonathan between my legs and his tasty lips on mine kissing me hungrily. He goes to my neck and my head falls back from the pleasure. My legs tighten around his waist bringing him closer if that is even possible. My breathing quickens. My hands make their way to his chest, then his back. I bite my bottom lip. Jonathan unbuttons my jeans and starts making circular movements on that tiny sensitive spot. A moan escapes through my lips. I find Jonathan's lips made of ecstasy and kiss them. "Cum for me, dear." He whispers near my ear. And just after that, a mind-blowing orgasm hits me. "Take me to bed." I whisper-moan.

Jonathan takes me in his strong hands and brings me to the bed. He hovers over me and I reach for his pants. He kisses me smiling, which makes me smile, too. I grab his huge member, move my hand up and down and he groans. He thrust in my hand moving to my neck and I smile. Then, out of sudden, he removes my hand and stands up. He takes off my jeans, leaving me in just my lingerie, and then he does the same with his clothes. He comes over me again and whispers, "I want to take this off later.", grabbing one boob. His other hand goes to my clitoris and starts making the same maddening movements. My back arches but then my phone starts ringing. Jonathan takes off one shoulder strap. "Don't answer!" He says but the ringing starts getting annoying.

He drops his head on my chest. "Pick up!" He says defeated and I grab my phone. "But we continue after that." I smile and nod. "Hello!" I say somehow annoyed and clear my throat. "Hi, Kar." I hear my best friend's voice. My face immediately brightens up. "Hi, Moni! How are you? Why are you calling?" I ask seeing Jonathan's expression. 'He is planning something.' "I'm fine. I wanted to hear from you. Since we haven't seen each other for quite a long time. What about you? You sound somehow groggy and ill-humored..." She says and I notice Jonathan coming closer to me. "No. I'm fine. I was just a little busy before you called." I say escaping the truth.

Jonathan smiles mischievously placing himself between my legs. "No!" I whisper-yell. "Are you sure you are okay with talking right now?" Monica asks me and at the same time, Jonathan opens my legs wider. "I'm fine. Don't worry. It's just that... there is one person here that is trying to make me crazy." I try to move away but he grabs me stronger. I bite my lips. "Isn't it like 8 AM in Sweden?!" She asks me while Jonathan removes the lower part of my lingerie. " Yeah. He came over yesterday but then an awful snowstorm was declared and we couldn't leave. And anyone will not be able to in the next eighteen hours." I explain watching Jonathan's movements. His head is between my legs and even though my efforts, he's not moving at all.

"Oh!" Jonathan kisses my inner thigh and my breath hitches. "So, you are locked in your house with a stranger or a friend?" She asks and then Jonathan licks my very sensitive part. "I am not sure," I say trying not to moan. "What does that mean?" Jonathan starts making amazing work with his tongue. "Well..." I start trying really hard not to sound as horny and wet as I am. "We met yesterday... but we are pretty close," I explain and bite my bottom lip. "And he's kinda friendly. Except for..." I take a deep breath. "...the moments he's driving me crazy. Oh, Moni, can we talk later? I have to do something!" I say tired of all the torture. "Sure! Bye!" She answers sounding a little confused. "Bye!" I reply and hang up the damn phone.

I moan with relief and pleasure. I flip us over and place myself in just the right place, so Jonathan's member enters me. My head falls back, Jonathan groans. "I'll rid your head off right after this!" I say and started moving up and down.

Chapter 6

I'm in the kitchen, preparing breakfast, eggs, spinach, and mushrooms. Jonathan disappeared somewhere along with Charlie. Balbina is eating. When I'm done, I walk around the cabin to search for them. But they are nowhere to be seen. Then it hit me. He must be kidding me! I grab my jacket and open the front door. And then I see Jonathan playing with Charlie in the huge snow. And the snowstorm has stopped. "Charlie! Come here, boy!" I say, a little shouting so he hears me. And Charlie, being a good boy, comes to me, all covered in snow. I smile. "Join us!" Jonathan says coming towards me. "Join you?! I was thinking of punching you in your pretty face!" He stands up in front of me and kisses my nose. "Relax! The snowstorm is taking a break. It's perfect for having fun and Charlie can spend some energy, so he sleeps all night. And..." He wraps his arms around my body. "... we can have some fun, too. Another kind of fun. Not that I don't like the idea of being with you in the bed, kissing every single-"

"I get it!" I interrupt him putting my hand over his mouth. He starts laughing and I smile. "So? Are you joining us?" I think for a moment. "Let me grab something warmer first," I answer and go back to the hallway. There I see Jonathan doing some weird movements with Charlie and a wide smile on his face. I laugh a little and put on a thick coat with a hood. I put on my boots and just when I go out a snowball hits my face. I clean it off and see Jonathan laughing coming to me. "Are you alright?" He asks me still laughing hard and helps me with the snow on my face. "Oh, I'm fine. But it's another question if you will be." I say and grab some snow. Jonathan runs away laughing and just when he takes snow in his hands, I throw the snowball I formed seconds ago and it goes straight to his ass. I burst out laughing when he shouts "You! Evil woman!".

He throws a ball but I kneel down and escape it. "Weak!" I shout and throw another snowball. And just when he stands up to shoot his own, the ball I sent hits his chest. He loses his balance and falls on his butt. "What the hell?!" I start laughing hard finding it hard to catch my breath. I grab another portion of snow and look at the spot where Jonathan was seconds ago. I raise my eyebrow and sharpen my hearing. I notice Charlie's fluffy tail. There are two options: he is really dumb or he thinks I'm dumb. I stand up and observe. "Charlie!" I call for him and he runs to me. "Where is he?" I ask him and Charlie looks at my left. I turn around and start walking slowly. I sense someone behind me, so I turn around, and noticing Jonathan I slide down between his legs and kick his ass pushing myself out. He turns towards my direction and places his hands on his hips. "Have you been in the Army or something?" He asks me. "Not exactly." I stand up. "Okay. Now I'm curious." He says and the next second he throws himself into me and we fall in the snow. "I got you! Finally!" I laugh.

Jonathan comes closer to kiss me but then Charlie appears and barks. We laugh and stand up. "I will have a serious conversation with you, my friend!" Jonathan says to Charlie looking and pointing his finger at him. Charlie barks again which makes me laugh. "Let's go inside. The breakfast is ready and it's starting to snow again." Jonathan nods. "Come on, Charlie," I say, clean the snow off Charlie and we enter the cabin. We take off the coats and sit in front of the fireplace to warm up. "So... about being in the Army..." Jonathan starts. "I haven't been. I am just trained." I answer simply. "Where?" He asks and I move my look from the fire to him. "Mostly in my training room. Or outside."

"Wait! So you are self-trained?!" I nod. "I was learning from videos. And since I love action movies, when I see something I want to be able to do, I practice until I do it." I explain playing with my hands. "Why did you decide to do this?" He asks me looking at my hands. "I wanted to be able to protect myself," I say and he looks at me. "I just don't like being dependable. And powerless." I stand up going to the table. "What exactly are you practicing?" Jonathan asks following me. "Kung-fu, Kickbox, gymnastics, shooting...stuff like that." I sit on one of the chairs and Jonathan does so on the chair next to mine. "But aren't you Zen Buddhist?!" He asks me. I look at him with frowned expression and confusion. I didn't think he's interested in my personality. "I am. But that doesn't mean I won't protect myself and the people I love when needed." We stay quiet for a while. "What about you?" I ask and Jonathan shoots me with a surprised look. "You asked something about me?! Okay. We have progress. Well, I am an atheist. I train Thailand Kickboxing, strength training, yoga for mobility, shooting, as you already know, tennis and much more. And, well, I would do everything to protect myself and my family, too. I'm still surprised you asked something about me."

"Well, I think it will be better to know something about the person who I sleep with," I say and look at his thinking face. "Okay," He says suddenly. "Get to know each other time." He turns towards me. I just stay looking at him. "Shall I start?" He asks and I nod. "Okay. I'm a night owl. I like attention. I have soy and peach allergy. I tend to be a little messy." He says and smiles somehow nervously. "I love cashews and almonds. But I hate bakery and milk. It makes me throw up. I like thrillers, comedy, horror and action movies. I love challenges, having fun and change because I get easily bored. I own a variety of businesses in the areas of science, health, technology and the filming industry. I own one island in the Atlantic ocean, near Mexico, and I love going there with friends and family. Your turn."

"Okay. I'm insomniac ever since I remember myself. I like everything to be in its own place, but I don't like detailed plans, I prefer having freedom and flexibility in my schedule. I get bored easily, too. And that's why many of my relationships ended when I think about it now. My businesses are in the areas of science, technology, and self-improvement. I love fruits, especially bananas, and yes, I realize it sounds bad. I hate being controlled, lies, small talks, drama, and people who make excuses and just complain." I grab the dishes and put them in the washing machine. "Oh, and..." I turn around. "I like your sense of humor and kinky side."

Chapter 7

I'm on my laptop, doing research for my next project on self-improvement which is about performance and productivity. I'm interrupted by my phone. "Hello?" I pick up without looking at who it is. "Hi! It's me, Taehyung!" I hear the voice of my best best friend from my phone. "Teddy Bear! I am so happy to hear from you! How are you?" I ask, close my laptop and stand up. "A little freezing right now. But I bet if you open the front door, I'll feel one hundred percent better!" He says and I frown. I step towards the window near the front door and look through it. My smile immediately grows when I see a man clothed in a long light brown thick coat, black jeans, and black winter shoes. I hang up and rush to unlock and open the door. "Teddy Bear!" I say loudly and hug him. "Princess!" He says hugging me. "I missed you so much!" I close my eyes. "Come on!" He takes off his shoes and coat and we sit on the sofa face to face. "How did you make it?" I ask looking into his deep brown eyes. "The snowstorm is not over! And the group. I thought you, guys, have a concert going on."

"We do. But, as you said there is a snowstorm, and we had to cancel. And I decided to check on you." He explains and I notice his new hairstyle. "Curly blonde... I like it! It suits you!" I say touching his hair a little. "Hey, I was wondering..." I hear Jonathan's voice coming from behind me. I turn around. "Nevermind. Who is the Asian guy?" He asks. "This is Taehyung. He is from a South Korean group, TAT. Taehyung, this is Jonathan." They shake hands. "I am the boyfriend!" Jonathan says and I shot him with a surprised look. 'We are dating?' He just smirks. "I am the best friend!" Tae says and looks at me. "공주님, 남자 친구가 있다고 언제 말하려고 했어요?" - When did you plan on telling me you have a boyfriend, Princess? - He asks me and I look at Jonathan. "남자 친구를 사귀 자마자 말해 줄게 하지만 몇 초 전에 이해했기 때문에 ..." - I would tell you immediately after getting a boyfriend. But since I understood it seconds ago... - I say looking from Jonathan to the ground and then Tae. "I see your Korean is still amazing." Teddy Bear says and I smile. "나는 수업을 그리워하지 않는다." - I never miss a lesson.

"Okay... I'll be in our bedroom." Jonathan says and I nod. "Okay," I answer looking at him with a thank you in my eyes. "So? How are the other boys?" I ask returning my whole attention to Tae. "Kyong is probably going from one to another making sure everyone is okay. You know him. Minjun is a little sick. Just flu, nothing serious. Jiho is probably in his room, studying. And Hyunwoo said that he is going to call his parents." Teddy Bear says and while doing so, we lay down on the sofa and cuddle. "When do you have to get back to them?" I ask, placing my head on his chest. "Tomorrow at 11 AM." He answers. I just stay silent for a moment. "I guess we have to make the most of our time together," I say finally and get up."Is he treating you well?" Teahyung asks me and I look at him with a raised eyebrow. "Are you seriously asking me this?"

"You look anxious. And you are far from relaxed." He sits up and I sign out. "Tell me what is it, Princess!" He says and I sit crossed-legs. "My family is coming over for Christmas. And, no it's not the far forgotten fear of my father or the rest of the family issues. I got over that and I have no intention of returning to it. It's just that they will meet with my biological father... And my mother and second father are not gonna like it. And on the top of all that, I still don't know if I have a boyfriend or not." I say and raise my eyebrows at the end of my sentence. "Everything is going to be fine." He hugs me. "You can cope with anything. You are my little ninja." I laugh a little. Then I stop and think for a few seconds. "Can you excuse me for a while? I want to solve one of the issues."I ask and look at him. "Go."

"Thank you!" I kiss his cheek and rush to the stairs and then in my bedroom. I open the door and see Jonathan with a book in his hands. "I confess that you have interesting taste in books." He says, closing and waving Bossy, one of my books. But he doesn't know that. No one, except for me and Tae, doesn't know because I use Kate White as a name for my books, except for the ones based on my companies' work. "Is this your type?" He asks and I look at him confused. "Type of ideal partner. Bossy, stubborn..." He starts. "No, no! I just like books like this. Whatever! I didn't come to talk about this." I sit on the couch next to the window. "Why did you tell Taehyung you are my boyfriend? I don't remember discussing that." I cross my arms.

Jonathan smirks. "Am I not your boyfriend or you sleep with guys just like that!?"

"I don't think you understand the situation properly," I say but am immediately interrupted. "Believe me. I do. I am just messing up with you. Whatever! I said that because I don't plan on just having sex with you, Karolina. And I usually get what I want." He finishes. "Okay," I just say and stand up. I leave the room and when I close the door, I take a deep breath. I am about to get going when the door is being opened and I am dragged by the arm back in the room. Suddenly I am pressed against the wall and Jonathan's lips are on mine. His hands go to my left breast and I bite my bottom lip. "Jonathan, we can't do this now!" I say protesting even though my body was quite clear about it wants. "Teahyung is downstairs." He stops. "What about tonight?" He asks me, his head on my pounding chest. "I want to spend time with him because he's leaving tomorrow morning."

"Jeez!" He mutters, rises and runs his hand through his perfect hair. "But tomorrow, after he leaves, you are mine." He kiss-bite my bottom lip. "I can't promise. My family should come tomorrow afternoon." I wrap my hands around his neck. "One hour. I will want your attention for one hour." He says and my heart somehow clenched. "Okay," I answer and kiss him gently.

Chapter 8

"Sorry for making you wait," I say, going towards the sofa. "It's nothing. Actually, I expected it taking much longer than that." I lie next to him. "I will pretend I didn't hear the second sentence," I say and feel his body shake a little because of his laughing. "Now, seriously. What happened?" He asks and I make myself come closer to his body. "He said he didn't plan on just sleeping with me. I suppose that means we are a couple now..." He hugs me tight. "Congratulations then, Princess!" I smile. "Thank you!... I guess." He pushes me a little. "Don't even dare to overthink! I think we should celebrate!" He says and smiles bright and wide. "But first, let's catch up. Tell me what's going on in your life, besides the new guy who ended up being your boyfriend."

"Okay. Well, I am writing a new book. Its name is Past Ghost. I think you will like it. It will be available in Korean, too. The companies are running great. And right now lots of people ask me questions about eating and fitness during the holidays..." I stop when I notice his look. "What?"I ask. "I'm asking about your personal life. When are you going to learn that?" He says kissing my forehead. I smile. "I'm sorry. Well, you know how things are. My family situation is getting better. I still think my second father is kind of a pain in the ass though. But my fear is fading away with time. My brother is still 50/50. Sister - well, the same crazy woman. And, as you already know, tell her something and the entire family knows after that. My mother... she may be a little uneducated, but I love her with my whole heart. I'm getting closer to my biological father and my other two brothers."He hugs me. "I'm happy for you. But I would like it if your second father stops acting as if he is God and starts caring for you." I frown. "I don't care that he doesn't care for me the way he does for my sister and brother." I look Tae into his eyes. "I just want him to shut his mouth up sometimes and act like a normal healthy person. Enough of this! Tell me about you!"

"Well, we are about to release a new album. And a new MV. But we need a girl for the video." He says and I look at him. "Oh?" I mumble and he nods. "And as always you were the first that came up on my mind, so I offered you... the manager wanted a picture and I showed him some. He liked you." I sit up. "Tae, I already told you, I don't think it's a good idea." I bite my lip and cross my hands. He sits up next to me and put his hands on both my shoulders. "You will be perfect for it! You are small, beautiful and cute!" I look at him with my skeptic's face. "And your personality and dance skills... you are perfect, Princess!" He hugs me from behind. "If I say 'yes' will you be happy?" I ask and he nods energetically. "Okay, then." He starts clapping and smiling. I smile, too. "We should really celebrate." He says and stands up. He opens the laptop and I go next to him. "You still have the 'Dance' playlist, right?" I nod. "I do." He hits the play button and the first song is BTS - Mic drop [Full-Length Edition]. Teddy Bear smiles widely. "I love this song."

"Me, too!" Then I see Jonathan going down the stairs. "I'm going to my cabin. See you tomorrow?" He asks coming to me and hugs me. "Of course!" I answer and wrap my hands around his waist. "If you need anything, come straight to my cabin. Or call me!" He says and places a kiss on my forehead. "Okay," I nod. He grabs his jacket, opens the door, waves and gets out. "What is it?" Tae asks me. I purse my lips. "Honestly, I have no idea what's going on. He's confusing me. At first, he seemed somehow bossy. Then he started acting all sexy and confident, even cocky at times. And now he's being all sweet and caring." I explain looking from the door to Tae. "Maybe he's opening up slowly." He says coming up to me. "You can talk with him about that later, now let's have fun."

Chapter 9

"I am tired. Can we go to bed?" Teddy Bear asks while throwing himself on the sofa. "Of course!" I say and grab his hand. "Let's go!" We start climbing the stairs slowly and lazily. "You know BTS would like you a lot." I look at him with a frowned face. "What's up with you lately?" I ask speeding up. "It just popped up in my mind when we were dancing." I nod. "Okay. I am going to take a quick shower, okay?" Taehyung nods and we enter into my bedroom. I enter the bathroom and hear my phone vibrate. I grab it and see that Jonathan texted.

Jonathan: I was gracefully welcomed!

I look at the picture where a little puppy is surrounded by all kind of ripped toys and even toilet paper and start laughing out loud.

Me: I already like him. :D

I put the phone down, take off my clothes, and turn on the shower with a wide smile on my face. I step in and then I feel the warm water on my shoulders. When I am done, I get out and go directly to the closet. I put on a pajama and dry my hair. I throw myself on the bed next to Tae who is scrolling on his phone. I go to the bathroom, just to get my phone, and then back on the bed. I open the message Jonathan sent minutes ago.

Jonathan: So you are taking his side...

Me: Of course! What did you expect?! He's so cute!

Jonathan: What about me?

I read and then look at the picture he sent seconds before the text. He's using the bunny filter from Instagram making his eyes bigger and his facial expression even cuter, and he is making a peace sign. I smile brightly. "Looks like someone special is texting you," Tae says, and I look at him. "Jonathan is sending me weird pictures." I show him the picture of Jonathan with the bunny filter. Then I see that he sent a second one, too. I open it and immediately regretted it by laughing really loud. He's obviously having dinner, but a small drop of sauce is flowing down from his lips. And he, honestly, is looking adorable. Then I see there is another picture sent by him. The drop is still there and he's making a weird face. "I really don't know what's up with that boy!" I say laughing and handing the phone to Teddy Bear. "Do you think he has a 4D personality?" Tae asks me. "I have no idea. I know him for less than a week. I guess I'm about to find out. I didn't even know he has a dog." I shake my head a little. Tae gives me back my phone.

Me: Okay, I confess! You are cute!

I look at the time, 11:28 PM, put my phone down and cuddle into Taehyung. "He is really weird..." I say and smile a little, then I yawn. "Can you sing something?" I ask and put my head on Tae's chest. "Okay," He answers and starts singing Someone like you. Soon after that, he goes quiet. I look up and see him sleeping. I grab my phone and see another text from Jonathan.

Jonathan: I'm bored. And I can't sleep.

Me: Me, too. And Taehyung is already asleep.

He answers immediately after I sent him the text.

Jonathan: FaceTime?

Me: If you want to.

Instead of replying, he is calling right away. I go out of the bedroom and pick up. "Hello, Mr. Charming!" I say seeing his handsome face. "Hello to you, too, beautiful! Where are you going?" He asks seeing me going around. "To the living room. I don't want to wake Tae up." I answer him with a smile. "Can't you go to your room?" He asks me when I sit on the couch next to the still warm fireplace. "No. Tae is sleeping in my room." I look at him examining his face. "It seems you are very close." He says looking at something next to him. "We are. We have been friends for three years now. And he has always been there for me even when we were apart. Don't worry about the fact that he's sleeping in my bed. He's like a brother to me."

"Okay," He answers simply and adjusts himself on the bed. "I wanted to ask you something," I say. "Go ahead." He tilts his head to the right. "During the first hours of our...umm... time together you were bossy, then you were sexy, then - funny and now you are acting all cute and charming. Do me a favor and tell me exactly what kind of a person you are because you are confusing me." I say watching his smirk appearing slowly on his face. "The things are getting interesting. Well, okay, let me explain." He sits up. "I don't put myself into any of the categories. I can be bossy and sexy, especially if it comes to being in the bed with you. I can be funny and goofy when I think it's appropriate. And I can be charming when I want to show pure love and the fact I care about someone. It all depends on the person and the situation. Does that answers your question, baby?" I nod. "Yes. And I like the answer."

Chapter 10

I wake up and look at my watch, 3:44 AM. Then I look at my phone and realize Jonathan and I are still on the video chat. "Hm..." I mumble but then I hear Jonathan's sleepy voice saying: "Don't hang up..." I smile a bit. "I won't!" I say wishing he was here. 'No! No! No! You don't! It has been less than a week!' And with these thoughts, I stand up and drink a glass of water. 'I am not sleepy, so I think of starting the day.' I run the coffee machine while thinking about how my sleep was the last few days. 'It has been pretty peaceful, but I have to sleep for more than 3 hours.' I think remembering I might have fallen asleep at about 1 AM while being on FaceTime with Jonathan. 'Hmm, thinking of whom... what do I find about him so that I let him so much in my space...'

The sound of the coffee machine spans me out of my thoughts and I pour the Kion coffee in my favorite Christmas cup. I smell it with my eyes closed. I love the smell of just prepared coffee and I've loved it since my early ages. It relaxes me and makes me think of a great Hawaiian rainy day with a cup of coffee and a book. Yeah, I will always love this combination! Still with the coffee in my hands, I go into my closet so that I can get in my workout outfit. I look at my reflection on the mirror. The girl I was many, many years ago wouldn't even dream of the way I look now since she thought she was short and not exactly in love with herself. But I put into the work and look at me now, I am 161 centimeters tall, skinny but fit and most importantly I love myself.

I grab my cup and head to the training room. "Ana, show me the plan for today!" I say to Ana, an AI robot and system that takes care of my needs and every single other person who had bought the same robot. Of course, every single system has its own name based on the person's taste. Ana shows me the schedule for today on the massive monitor in the center of the room. I start by setting up the atmosphere for meditation. I dim the lights, light up the aroma candles, and turning on today's melody. Birds singing along with the sound of bubbling water. Just perfect. After an hour-long meditation, I warm up and start running on the treadmill while listening to my workout playlist. "Miss, you have a message from Jonathan," Ana informs me. "Screen look on the monitor."

Jonathan: Where did you go?

"Ana, connect the video chat with monitor number 3 in the training room!" I say so that I can talk with Jonathan while running. After a second, Jonathan's face is on the screen before me. "Good morning to you, too!" I say to him. "Good morning! Did you sleep at all?" He asks me. "I did," I answer him simply. "Seriously?! Because you woke up at about 4 AM. And the nights before you woke up at least two times. This is not normal..." I roll my eyes. "It's nothing. Don't worry! I just sleep lightly." I speed up a little. "You didn't sleep at all, too. You even told me not to hang up..."

I say looking at him. He just nods looking somehow lost in thoughts. Then I hear a rude male voice, "Jonathan... what are you doing?". "I will see you later. Okay?" I nod. What was that?

I finish my workout and go to take a cool shower. As I step in the water, my thoughts start pacing up. 'The man that came in Jonathan's room sounded like a not so polite man. I wonder who was that... Could it be his father... Whatever, it's not my business. I just hope it's nothing terrible.' After that, my thoughts take a different direction. I start thinking about a new idea for my book. Then an idea for my business appeared. I get out of the shower and write down my ideas, so I can implement them later. I get into a black blouse and black skinny jeans and do my hair into a messy bun. I look at my watch and see it's 6:12 AM. 'Tae will not wake up until 9... So, I'll start preparing for when my family will come after I finish my routine.'

I go downstairs and grab the book sitting on the left side of the sofa. I am all caught up on the book and so when someone puts a hand on my shoulder, I catch it and twist it. "Ah! Calm down! It's me!" Jonathan says trying not to show that his wrist hurts. "I'm sorry!" I apologize, letting go of his hand. "No problem. I'll know for the next time..." He says and sits next to me. "What are you so caught up on, so that you didn't hear the bell ringing?" He asks taking the book from my hand. "Boundless: Upgrade Your Brain, Optimize Your Body & Defy Aging - Ben Greenfield... It is a really great book. I read it two months ago." I look at him with curiosity, and maybe a little hope, in my eyes. 'I think I found a reason to like him even more.' "What?" He asks and I move my eyes off him. "Nothing," I answer but then he places his hand on my chin and moves my face so that I face him.

His face was just an inch or so away from mine. I look carefully at his face, somehow examining his face. Now when he's so close to me I see his eyes are generally brown, but there is a slight note of gold in them. Then my eyes move to his lips. They were thin, now distorted in a mischievous smile, and Gosh were they perfect! I bite my bottom lip, but then he smashes his delicious lips on mine. My body goes on fire immediately. Just like the night, he kissed me for the first time. My hands wrap around his neck and I let myself enjoy the moment. His hungry kisses and his right hands on the side of my hips, his left one on my cheek. Jonathan slowly and carefully lays me down. His right hand goes under my blouse and my breath hitches letting a small moan escape my mouth. Jonathan groans a little and positioned himself between my legs pressing himself closer and closer to my heated body.

My breath quickens and when his boner touches my inner thigh, a soft very quiet moan escapes my lips. His hand goes up to my breast while his lips make their way down to my neck. I bite my lips but then I hear, "OMG, I'm so sorry!". Jonathan removes his hand from my breast and stops kissing me but doesn't move away from between my legs. We look up to the stairs, from where the sentence came seconds ago and see Taehyung covering his hands and claiming the stairs back to the second floor. I throw my head back and my body starts shaking from a silent laugh. Jonathan drops his hand on my chest. "I can't believe it!"

He murmurs and I continue laughing silently. "I am taking you tonight at my house!"

"I am sorry, but I think this can't happen," I say and run my hand through his silky black hair. "My family will be here tonight!" I explain to him before he asks. Jonathan lifts up his head and looks right into my eyes. "But... I still have time left until I start preparing the dishes. But I want to spend some more time with Taehyung. That's why you have an hour." His eyes fill up with joy. Or at least that is what is more visible. Behind the spark of joy, there is something else and this thing is lust.

Chapter 11

After hearing that we have an hour, in which we are free to do what we weren't able to for some time, Jonathan starts kissing me slowly but then the slow kiss turns into a passionate one. I open my eyes remembering that Taehyung may come again. "Don't worry about your friend. I don't think he'll come again!" Jonathan says placing his hand on my hip. "I offer you to go to the bedroom you were supposed to sleep in." He takes me in his hands and I wrap my legs around his waist. "As you wish." He says and gives me a quick kiss. He starts claiming the stairs and I take my chance to kiss and nip on his neck. "Wait for the bedroom," he moans a little and I smile and continue kissing. But then, all of sudden he stops and puts me against the wall smashing his lips on mine. My head spins and I strengthen my hold on him.

I hear a ripping of cloth and soon realize that was my blouse. I unwrap my legs and push myself out of the wall so that I can lead to the bedroom. When we reach the bedroom, he takes the lead and brings us both down on the bed. He takes off his t-shirt and hovers over me again smashing his lips on mine once again and kissing me hungrily. I have never even dreamt of someone kissing me like this. I wrap my legs around him making him come closer to my body. I feel his boner on my lower abdomen and reach out for his jeans. He immediately removes my hands. "Not so fast!" He says with his sexy turning on raspy voice making my knees go weak. Jonathan bites my bottom lip, then kissing and nipping he makes his way down to my breast. With one move my bra is thrown away and his lips are on my nipple. I moan, "Jonathan..." and he groans.

He comes on my lips again and whispers, "Don't move!". I snap open my eyes and look at him and the smirk he has on his beautiful face. *Why is this turning me on*? I question myself. I nod and Jonathan starts making his ways down slowly kissing every single part of my body and setting me fire. He unbuttons my jeans, takes them off and throws them away just as he did with my bra. He kisses my womanhood through my panties sending me chills from pleasure. A moan escapes my lips and I bite my lip hard. Jonathan spreads out my legs and places himself between them. He kisses my inner thighs slowly, almost torturing. One of his hands suddenly goes above my clit and I shut my eyes close when he does ungodly things to me down there. "Jonathan!" I moan a little bit louder. He stops, removes my lace panties, and slowly, really slowly licks my now very wet and sensitive part. Then he flicks his tongue and I almost scream his name. "Be more quiet, baby!"

I bite my lips letting myself feel every single flick, lick, and kiss he places on my body. Along with that, his hands are on my hips holding me strongly. He flicks one more time and I feel tightening and then I see stars. *Am I dreaming?!* I ask myself. Jonathan comes over to my lips and kisses me passionately. I push him aside and come over him. I kiss him moving my hands down to his jeans to unbutton them. I broke the kiss and Jonathan helps me with taking off the jeans along with his boxers. I bite my bottom lip when I see just how much he is turned on. I grab his huge member carefully and lick it just as slowly as he did to me. He hisses, grabs my hand, and looks me right into the eyes. His eyes are darkened and the lust is obvious. I take in his cock slowly while looking at his eyes. He throws his head back while groaning. I start moving my hand and head up and down giving him the best I can do. He moans, looks at me and groans. I liked it every single time he did it. But then he stops me and tosses me to his side coming over me.

Jonathan looks at me and while doing so he stands up, grabs a condom, puts it on him, and comes back at me. "Look at me!" Jonathans says and I do as I'm told. Then while staring at my eyes, swimming into my soul, he enters me slowly filling me up. I close my eyes enjoying the fullness. "Open your eyes, baby!" Jonathan whisper-moans and I open them. He starts moving in and out slowly. *He wants to make love, not sex.* And with this single thought, I kiss him letting my hands go all over his body while his strong hands are doing the same to me. He looks me into the eyes again but speeds up. I moan and he speeds up even more until the whole bed is shaking and I feel my walls tightening around his dick. Then, some more thrusts and my second orgasm hit me like a wave. Jonathan keeps moving in and out and me in harmony with his moves. He kisses me, grabs me tighter, and puts his head on the crook of my neck. Two thrusts and he goes numb on me.

Jonathan gets his head up and looks at me, peering his eyes into my soul. He kisses me and lays down by my side. I am about to reach for the blanket but then Jonathan's hand stops mine. "Please... don't cover yourself..." I look at him.* I know there is no way to be cold here, but...* He just moves his hand from my hand to my waist and moves me closer to him, so I cuddle into him. Jonathan kisses my neck and then my lips. "You are so beautiful..." he whispers near my ear. I look at him and run my hand through his messy hair. I give him a peck. He looks at me and kisses me deeper. His tongue enters my mouth ready to explore and his body comes on the top of mine. He positioned himself between my legs, his right hand going up and down on my thigh while his left is caressing my chin. "Karolina..." Jonathan whisper-moans making his way to my neck turning me on even more. I bite my lip. Then I feel Jonathan's hand, the one that has been on my thigh second ago, on my clit. I let out a moan. *Here comes the second round.*

Chapter 12

I breathe in and out heavily. If the first round was ungodly great, the second was on a universal level. I still don't know how he knows how to make my knees go weak with just one touch, but he does it and how big fat lie would it be if I say I don't like it! And on top of that, he's extremely intelligent, smart, sexy, and funny. It's like the Universe sent him to me. But when I think about all that, I want to close myself and push him away because of the last time I thought like that. It all seemed perfect until the bastard started trying to control me and acting needy. Jonathan's touch on my cheek snaps me out of my thoughts. "What are you thinking about?" He asks me and I look away. "Nothing important!" I answer and sit up. "It isn't nothing if it distances you from me!" Jonathan fights back. "I don't know who hurt you in the past..." I stop him with a quick kiss.
"Save it!" I say and he frowns. I try to move away but Jonathan grabs me and puts me down on the bed coming over me. "No! You'll listen to me!" He kisses me fiercely. "I have been hurt, too, Karolina! I know what it's like your heart to be broken and I won't do the same! I'll not hurt you! I just want to get to know you on an even deeper level. And I'm not just talking about the positive stuff. I want the bad stuff, too! I want to understand all that while having you in my arms, in the bed, and by my side! And I'll not give up! Not just because I want it! But because I see you want it,

too! I see it every time I come into the room. I see it every time I kiss you and I see it every time I'm inside you! So you better prepare your guarded heart for an attack!" He finishes and I just look at him. I'm looking at him with fury, respect, and passion at the same time.

Jonathan moves away from me and grabs his boxers. I stand up, turn him around, and wrap my hands around his neck just to kiss him. "I thought you wouldn't do anything!" Jonathan says with a smile on his face. "I thought that, too. But now, I'm not letting you go!" I say looking straight into his eyes.* He wasn't lying! No one can talk like that if he or she is lying! No one!* He smiles and walks me back to the bed where we fall. Still, with a smile on his face, he hugs me tightly, very tightly.* I haven't been hugged like this for years!* I thought and hug him back taking in his smell and warmth. "Now I don't want to leave. Can I help you prepare for tonight?" I nod. "May I invite my father?" He asks me and my eyes snap open. "Don't look at me like that! I want to introduce you! My father is an essential person in my life, and I think he's gonna like you."

Okay, then. But that means I have to go to the grocery once again." I say and Jonathan gives me a quick kiss. "I will do that! You spend some time with your friend. Just tell me what I have to get." I smile and nod. He kisses me and is about to break the kiss but I deepen it. He smiles. "Don't you dare move away from me!" I say and Jonathan moves us up on the bed so we can be comfortable. "As you wish, darling!" He says and we kiss. The kiss is deep, full of passion and love. I place one of my legs on the top of his and let my hands go examine his fit upper body. All the muscles are carefully taken care of and I feel it as I touch every single part of his body. "You are gonna be late!"

Jonathan says with his raspy voice, meaning he's just as turned on as me. "I'll manage with your help," I say and in the next moment, his lips are back on mine.

"I don't have any more condoms..." Jonathan whispers. "Guess you have one more reason to go shopping," I say with a smile on my face. "Let's start getting ready!" I say and we get up. Then I stop. "What?" Jonathan asks me and I look at him wide-eyed. "Taehyung!" He just keeps looking at me confused. "He must be traumatized!" I say putting hands on my head and laughing quietly. "What do you mean?" Jonathan asks me still confused but with a wide smile on his face. "Well, we weren't exactly quiet..." I answer him and he laughs. "I'm sure he has heard things like that before," Jonathan says, winks and hugs me. "You are right. But just think about it... you in your friend's house and hearing her having sex... I wouldn't want to experience that." I say shaking my head. "You can talk with him later. Let's take a shower now." Jonathan says grabbing my hand heading me to the bathroom. "Yeah, but you forget about something."

"What?" He asks when we enter the bathroom. "There are no towels here and you ripped most of my clothes. This means I can't go to my bedroom and take towels and new clothes." I explain noticing his smirk *when I mention the part of my clothes being ripped by him. I honestly thought that happens only in the books and the movies.* I think, raising my eyebrow. "I'll take the towels," Jonathans says and kisses my forehead. He gets out of the bathroom. "Don't forget to put on something," I say peaking my head from the bathroom. "Are you worried he's gonna see me?" He asks with a smirk forming on his precious lips. "I'm more worried about him," I say looking at Jonathan from head to toe. *Yeah, he has a body of a God!* I think and immediately try to change the topic that appeared in my mind. Jonathan laughs asking me "Why so?".

"Reasons," I say and realize it sounded even more mocking than it should immediately after seeing Jonathan's look darkening. "Are you on birth control?" He asks me and I look at him wide-eyed. *I'm in trouble*. "Yes," I whisper and nod when I understand it was too quiet for him to hear my answer. After that, he puts on his boxers and gets out. *How much sex is too much sex?* Questions appear on my mind. *And how does it happen that one day you literally have no sex life and the next you have sex for an entire week?* The door opens and I see Jonathan with two towels in hand. He closes the door and comes right to me smashing his lips at me. Sorry, Tae! I kiss Jonathan back and like this, we enter the bathroom. We broke the kiss just to turn on the water. Right after that, my back is pressed against the bathroom's wall and Jonathan is kissing me hungrily. I moan and he picks me up. I wrap my legs around him pressing him closer to my body feeling his heartbeat. It's rapid just like mine.

Jonathan's hand goes on my hip and then I feel him entering into me. I close my eyes enjoying every single inch entering, widening, and filling me in. "Mmm..." I let out a small moan from pleasure. "You're driving me crazy!" Jonathan groans and starts moving in and out of me. We moan and kiss. He goes to my neck while I trail my hands all over his upper body. "You're mine!" Jonathan says and with one more thrust, I come. Jonathan moves in and out a few more times, then out, and comes all over my stomach. We breathe heavily, our foreheads in touch, warm water falling on our bodies. I really thought this kind of thing happens only in books, movies, and your imagination. But obviously, they really exist. And I'll admit, I love it!

Chapter 13

"Don't be like this! I said I'm sorry!" I say trying to hug Taehyung who is crossing his arms and has been like this since Jonathan left and we were left alone. Then he smiles. "Aigo! How can you think I am mad at you?" He says and hugs me. "This is truly impossible!" He says almost shouting and laughs. "It's not funny! I thought you were really mad at me!" I make a step back. "For what? For enjoying some time with the person you obviously have fallen for?" He asks and I feel some blood rushing to my cheeks. "OMG! You're blushing!" Taehyung says pointing at me with a big smile on his face. "I know you for years and you haven't blushed even once!" I look at him trying to appear serious. "I'm not blushing! You're just imagining!"

"Tell this to your pretty red face!" He says grabbing me by the shoulders and putting in front of the mirror in the living room. I look at myself and more specifically at my tomato face. "It's just hot in here..." I make a stupid excuse. Taehyung mumbles something and looks away. "Huh?" I ask and his look comes back to me. "I said, I wonder why!" I look at his reflection on the mirror, turn around and pinch his arm. "You, pervert boy!" He starts laughing. "Well, I wouldn't say anything if it wasn't for all the noise I heard earlier!" I pinch him again, he screams and laughs again. "You're just unbelievable!" I say making my way to the couch and throwing myself into its softness. "Yeah, it's me who is unbelievable..." I grab a pillow at throw at him. "What the fuck happened to you?!" I shout. "You took away my purity!" He shouts from the other corner of the room. "You just signed up for early death!" I stand up ready to catch him and Taehyung runs up the stairs laughing. I go after him.

I hear a door opening and rush back the living room shouting, "You're mine after a minute!". I hear Taehyung's laugh and a wide smile appears on my face. I see Jonathan taking off his thick coat. I notice the movement of every muscle and that he changed his clothes. Tight black blouse, making his muscles even more visible. Jeans, perfectly fitting his body. "You okay?" Jonathans asks snapping me out of my thoughts. I notice I have been leaning against the wall, my hand on my chin, and biting my bottom. "Um..." I clear my throat. "Yes, I am!" I answer and straighten my posture acting as if I haven't been drooling over him seconds ago. I go to him and grab one of the bags. "I thought I mentioned fewer things than that..." I say looking at the four bags full of groceries and some other things I couldn't recognize through the bags' material. "You did. But I bought some stuff... among others." I move my look away. Jonathan smirks.

Sometimes I wonder, do I want to smack his face or kiss him until... Stop! I stop myself from going further. "You sure you're okay? You seem a little red and... deep in thoughts." Jonathan says and kisses my forehead. I nod. "You'll tell if there's something. Right?" He asks me and again, I nod. "I just need to take care of something...

someone first. Give five minutes maximum!" I say showing my hand for five. Jonathan smiles. "Okay." I turn around and rush up the stairs. "Teahyung! I'm coming!" I shout coming right into the bedroom. But he is not there. I turn around and see him coming right to me. Then he trips and falls over me which makes me fall, too, on the ground. "You know... sometimes I wonder how you can be so clumsy," I say with my eyes closed. Taehyung moves to my side slowly.

I get up quickly and give a hand to Taehyung. "What do you plan on doing? Cooking with me and Jonathan or something?" I ask him, getting out of the bedroom. "Cooking with you is always fun." Taehyung answers and I remember the last time cooking with him. It was a year and a half ago and we were in Korea for a few days so that I could spend some time with him. We decided to cook for ourselves, and, oh God, was it a disaster?! It all ended up with a messy kitchen - literally the whole kitchen along with me and Taehyung were covered in almond flour - and my injured middle finger. "Yeah... well, we all have luck I have improved my cooking skills. And I hope this time no one will be injured."

Chapter 14

'Last Christmas' is playing in the whole house while we are mostly dancing and singing. "I think turning on Christmas music was an awful idea," Jonathan says and I smile brightly at him singing. "No! It was the best idea!" I say and throw some flour on his face. With closed eyes, he grabs me and rubs his head on my chest. I laugh looking at Taehyung. "Help!" I shout for help but Tae just shakes his head. "Hello! The guy is pure muscles! I have no chance!" Taehyung says and I laugh even harder. Jonathan stops and looks at me. Then 'All I want for Christmas is you' starts playing and I look at the person who played it on. "I love this song and you know it!"

My look goes back to Jonathan's dark eyes. After that, I just feel his soft lips on mine. My whole body pins itself on his taking in the warmth and the scent. When he breaks the kiss, we hear Taehyung's voice, "And that is your first Christmas photo!". He shows us a picture on his phone, taken a moment ago, of us kissing. "First?" Jonathan asks looking at me. "He takes a lot of pictures," I answer instead of Taehyung. My phone starts ringing and I move a few steps away from Jonathan. "Let's get back to cooking!" I say answering the phone and grabbing the knife to finish chopping the carrots. "Hi, Erica!" I say but hear only heavy breathing and silent crying. I stop chopping and focus.

"Erica?"

"Kar, please, help me! He's coming for me!" Erica, one of my very best friends, says, her voice low and breaking. "Erica, where are you?" I ask worried and hurry to take my jacket. "Skansvägen street." She whispers in answer. "I'm coming!" I grab my keys for my white Tesla Model 3 Long Range. "What is it?" Taehyung asks. I just look at him while putting on my coat. I open the door in a hurry and rush to the car. I say the address and soon I'm on the road. "Erica? You still there?" I ask looking at the mirror. I notice the car behind me. "I am!" She answers quietly. "Okay. I will be there in less than two minutes. "Okay," she cries out and I focus on the road.

Just after a minute, I stop in the middle of the road covered in at least fifteen centimeters snow. I get out of the car. "Erica, I'm here," I say looking around. I hear a scream and run to where the sound came from. I see a woman, probably Erica, and a huge man right above her grabbing her and hitting her. I run in the snow and punch the guy right in the face. He falls on the ground and looks at me very surprised. "Bitch!" He shouts. I look at Erica and give her a hand. "Here!" I say giving her my coat seeing she is wearing only leggings and a thin blouse. "Go to the car!" I look at the bastard who is now getting up. "Kar..." Erica hesitates. "I said, go!" And she does so, running slowly and making her way to my car where. The man grabs my hand with one hand and my throat with the other. I push kick him in his chest with all my strength making some distance between us. I rotate myself and unload my foot on his face making him fall again. He groans in pain.

I turn around in order to go to the car but my ankle is grabbed by the man and I fall on my hands. The man comes above me, hovering over me, and swangs at my face. I move my head to the side and entangle my left leg above his elbow and below his armpit. I push kick his face with my other leg and rush to stand up. Then I see another person, someone tall with middle-length hair and a long coat, coming right to me. When the person comes closer, I see who he is. Jonathan. He looks at me, on all fours position, and then he moves his eyes, probably to face the man I was fighting with. "Oh, bro, your face is so fucked up! Let me help you repair it!" He says and punches the guy. The huge man falls once again on the ground. I stand by Jonathan's side and look at the gorilla. I smile. Jonathan grabs my face gently and examen it. I remove his hand and step forward. "Let's go!"

I open the car door and sit behind the wheel. "How are you?" I ask Erica while taking the turn so that we go to my place. She breaks down in tears. The whole road was taken in silence, except for the quiet sobbing from Erica. I get out of the car and help Erica who is covered in bruises. We enter the house and I help her lay on the sofa. "Taehyung! Give me the bag with the medicine!" I say and Taehyung goes up the stairs. Jonathan comes to me with two blankets. He gives the first to me and I wrap Erica in it, the second one he places on my shoulders. I take it off and put it aside. Taehyung comes back and gives me the bag. I open it and take some cotton, liquid iodine, cleanser for wounds, and arnica gel. I look at her. Her red hair is messy and wet, her petite body is still shaking and her lips are still blueish.

"Let's go to my room," I say, putting the things back in the bag, and help her stand up. I grab the bag with my other hand and we climb the stairs slowly. I turn my head over my shoulder just to look at Jonathan. He seems as though he wants to get up from the couch, his eyes directly looking into mine, his hands on the sides of the couch, and his muscles tightened. I look forward and we take the turn for my room. I place Erica on the bed and take her hair up in a light and a messy bun. "Tell me what happened!" I say to her while taking some cotton and the cleanser. "Greg..." She starts. *So, that was the name*. "He... I and Natasha... were walking towards the grocery to buy some things for our cake. The cake we make every Christmas. Then someone called her" she sobs and hitches when I start taking care of her wounds.

"She said her boss told her to send files he has been asking for or she would get fired. So she had to head home and do her job while I am buying the grocery needed for the cake and some other stuff. And when I entered the store I saw Greg. I hurried to get out..." She sobs again and wipes away her tears. "But he caught me and slapped me." I frown. "Why?" She looks up at me with her teary red eyes. "He still thinks I am responsible that he got caught by the police." *Right! He was caught with drugs enough for an entire state!* She answers and I nod giving her a sign to continue. "I escaped his grip and started running. And just like this some times. He would catch me, beat me up... until I decided to call you. And then, you appeared just on time. Otherwise..." She breaks down in tears. I leave the cotton away and take her in my embrace. "Don't think about that! What's important now is that you're safe. But we should probably contact Natasha." She gets away from the hug and looks me in the eyes. "You are right! I should have got home a long time ago. She must be so worried..." Erica says obviously tired. "Let me talk to her after I finish with your bruises and wounds. You should rest!" Erica nods and gives me her phone.

Chapter 15

"How is she?" Taehyung asks me. "She's fine. After I took care of her wounds, gave her clean and warm clothes, and talked with her girlfriend, she fell asleep. And I bet nothing can wake her up now." I smile a little.* She may be okay, but I am kinda worried about Jonathan. He hasn't opened his mouth since he punched Greg*. "Are you okay?" Taehyung's question snaps me out of my thoughts. "Mhm..." I mumble and take the stair to the living room where I see Jonathan deep in thoughts. "If you continue being this quiet, you will make me call my therapist." I sit next to him. "What's wrong?" I ask truly curious. "It's nothing. I just don't know how to help or even react. I am really bad at situations like this one."

"You reacted just fine for me. You came, even though I didn't want your help, punched the guy with a great note before that." He looks at me and I give him a warm smile. "But I didn't show any emotional support..." I stopped him with a hand over his lips. "You did great. You may talk with Taehyung about that, he will explain to you things I am not able to about this... Anyway, I don't need you to do things you don't want to do or don't know how to do. But if you want help and learn about how to do something, you can always ask me. And even if can't help you with this particular thing, I'll find a professionalist who can help you." He looks at me somehow suspiciously. *I expected a different reaction... Something feels off.* I think and then a wave of breathlessness washes over me. "Excuse me!" I stand up but Jonathan's hand grabs mine. Not now! "I am sorry! I am just not used to-"

"Jonathan, we will talk later. I just want to be alone for a while." I rip my hand off his and rush through the front door. The cold, almost freezing air surrounds me and I start taking deep breaths. "This can't be happening!" I whisper to myself and feel myself shaking. "Please!" I pray. But then my legs abandon me and I fall on my knees. I take a deep inhale and slowly exhale. "Calm down! Everything is fine!" I repeat a mantra to show my body everything is just great. "I am powerful! I can do anything! No one can hurt me!" I choke. No! I scream internally and sob. "Don't even dare to cry! You can NOT be weak!" I command myself. "Stand up and dry your face! Then you go in all calm and continue with preparing for this damn Christmas!" With all my willpower, I stand up. I take a deep breath and brush off my tears. I smile. Then I open the door and enter the house. I see Taehyung, who was probably about to open the door, in front of me with a hand in the air.

"Are you okay? Jonathan said you looked pale and rushed out!" He places his hands on my shoulders. "Why would I not be fine?" I ask with a smile. I remove his hands from me. "Let's continue with the preparing for Christmas!" I say moving aside from him. They both keep looking at me. "Teddy Bear, did you seriously thought I would give in?" I ask him with a teasing tone of my voice. He smiles. "Okay then." He hugs me. "You worried me!" I tap him on the back. "You shouldn't worry about me anymore."* I'm sorry, Tae! But you really should stop worrying about me*. He lets go of me and heads towards the kitchen plot. Jonathan comes to me. "Even I noticed you have lied and I am usually not aware of people's emotions." I frown acting all innocent. "Don't try that on me." He says with a stop hand-sign in front of my face. " You may have convinced him but I know something is wrong. I will not force you. You can tell me when you are ready." He locks his eyes with mine. I feel tears arising but I swallow and take a deep breath in. I smile and hug him. *You may look like a bad boy and say whatever you want to, but you are still amazing!*

Chapter 16

"They are going to be here any minute!" I say putting my phone back in my pocket. "We better hurry! Jonathan, what are you doing?" I ask seeing him next to the Christmas tree. "Nothing," he answers, turning around with his hands behind his back and an odd but beautiful smile on his face. I raise my eyebrow. "Really?" I move closer to him and take what's in his hands. "Who is this for?" I ask looking at a little bag for presents. I look up at him and his defeated face. I tilt my head to the right. "It is for you... but you are not opening it until tomorrow!" He says grabbing the back. He places it under the Christmas tree. I look at him with a smile. "I don't remember us discussing this. Probably this is the reason why you have done that."

"What do you mean?" He asks obviously confused. "She doesn't like being given presents." Taehyung answers instead of me. "You don't?" Jonathan asks not moving his eyes off me. "I don't. But, you can always give it to someone who is in need." I smile and place my arm on his shoulder. "Why do you not like presents?" I swallow hard and lick my lips. "It's a long story. I will come after a minute or so." I pat him and rush up to the second floor. "Why is she always rushing to somewhere today?" I hear Jonathan asking himself. "Well..." Taehyung starts and I stop just before the turn. "This day has never been easy for her. But that's not my story to tell." *Thank you!* I thank Tae in my head for being the best friend he has always been. "Hmm... does she link this day to something tragic?" Jonathan asks showing his obviously curious nature.

"Look, if she wants to tell you about this, she will. But, yes. Something bad happened on this day years ago." I see Jonathan turning around with determination. I stand up and enter my bedroom. I start box breathing. 4 seconds in, hold for 4 seconds, 4 seconds exhaling, 4 seconds hold. Then Jonathan comes in. "Are you okay?" He asks. I nod. "I am. Don't worry!" He looks at me suspiciously. "What happened on this day to you years ago?" He asks me directly. "Woah..." I can only say before he grabs me and kisses me. "You can trust me!" I nod taking a step back. I sit on the edge of my bed and Jonathan does so next to me immediately after that. "Look, I can't tell you some things. And it's not about trust, it's about the fact I don't want to recall them. And this particular thing hurts. A lot." I say looking straight into his eyes. "I hope you understand me." I lip my dry lips and take a deep breath. "I am trying to understand..." Here comes the 'but'. "But you wanna know?" He nods. Silence. "Okay," I take one more deep breath. "I'm gonna tell you." I reposition myself so I am more comfortable. "On this day, three years ago, happened way too many things. First, I got in an awful fight with my now ex-boyfriend," and just by the thought of that, tears start forming in my eyes and I form a fist.

"Stop!" Jonathan says wiping away a small tear on my cheek. "I don't want you to cry. If only I knew it is hurting you that much..." He hugs me but I just shake my head. "It's okay.

We both were crying at the end of it, and it ended with a leaving. After that, I told mom. She said I am the one responsible for it all, and so I had an argument with her, too. While arguing we forgot about the chicken in the oven and we would set on fire the whole house. And again she made me responsible for that, too. It was really bad. And so I decided to go out to take some fresh air." I stop and feel my jaw clenching. "While I was walking, I met a few guys who obviously were high and drunk. They were whistling after me and since I didn't pay any attention to them, they followed me." Jonathan's body tenses. "After a minute or so, one of them grabbed me by the hand and told me that we could have some fun. I would puke. I just shook my hand and went away. But then..." Jonathan's grip tightens.

"They surrounded me and tried to get closer to me. I got even angrier and kick one of the guy's balls. The second guy called a bitch and came closer but then I smashed his ugly face and did the same with his balls. I told them a thing or two and got rid of two more of them right after that. Then, the guy I kicked first stood up and with two other guys started coming closer. I ran directly to home and I had the luck I was just half a kilometer away. When I got home, I told my parents. My father got furious and we both went out, so I could show them to him. And well, it didn't end up well for the guys. Since that day, I don't want any presents, just my loved ones. And I always give as much as I can to a charity. That's why my company for female empowerment exits, too." Jonathan hugs me tighter. I let out the breath I was holding and turn to face him. "Thank you for telling me. I really prefer you to be open and honest rather than lie to me or hide from me. Even if the truth is harsh and I don't like it."

"Well, that's good for you. Because if you are part of my life, you have to know that it's either the raw truth or I am silent." He smiles. After that, I feel his lips on mine. "I will go with that." He says and just when he is about to kiss me again we hear voices coming from down the stairs. "My family..."

Chapter 17

"Мамо!" - Mom! - I say while throwing myself into my mother's arms. "Липсваяше ми!" - I missed you! - I look at my second father and hug him with a smile. "Здравей!" - Hello! - I look around for my brother and sister. "Къде са тези пакостници?" - Where are these trouble makers? - I ask looking at my mother. "Навън. Ей сега идват." - Outside. They're coming in awhile. - I nod. Then a snowball meets my stomach. "They got you," Jonathan says reminding me of his presence. "О, мамо, забравих. Това е Джонатан. Jonathan, that's my mother, Таня." - Oh, mom, I forgot. This is Jonathan. Jonathan, that's my mother, Tanya. - I introduce them. My brother and sister come in with luggage in their hands. I hug my little sister and brother. "За добре дошли със снежна топка ме посрещнахте." - As a welcome, you met me with a snowball. - I laugh a little. "Нямаше как иначе." - There was no other way. - My brother says. "Уха, ако бяхме говорили по телефона, нямаше да те позная." - Wow, if we were talking on the phone, I wouldn't recognize you. - I say a little surprised by how his voice changed.

"This is not Russian..." Jonathan says behind me. "It's Bulgarian. It's quite a long story. I will tell you everything later, okay?" He nods. "By the way, this is my sister, Viktoria. And my brother, Peter. This is Jonathan." He shakes hands with them. "You can talk with them in English." He smiles a little and kind of relaxes when he understands that. "It's my pleasure to meet you." He says politely and I look at him with a smirk. "What?" He asks when he notices my facial expression. "Are you trying to impress them?" Jonathan comes closer to me. "I don't think this will be necessary. I naturally charming." He whispers and I smile. "Okay. Хайде влизайте навътре. Настанявайте се!" - Come on, get inside. Make yourself comfortable! - I say a little louder. Everyone takes their shoes off and puts the luggage aside. "Ако някой е много гладен, той или тя може да намери почти всичко в хладилника. Може и да си сложите багажа по стаите." - If anyone is very hungry, he or she can find almost everything in the fridge. You can put your luggage in your room, too. - I announce and see Taehyung talking to my mother.

And she didn't like Asians before. I think for a second. *Taehyung did great by deciding to learn at least the basis of Bulgarian, too. Otherwise, now they wouldn't be even this close.* I smile. "What's in your pretty head?" Jonathan asks coming towards me. "I just thankful that my mother gets along with Taehyung better," I answer him still with my eyes turned to the direction of my mother and my best friend. "You know, I find your family funny just by the first minutes with it." I laugh. "Oh, you haven't seen even the little things." I pat him on the shoulder. "What does that mean?" He asks me. "I will let you see it for yourself." My attention goes to Viktoria. "Како, къде е тоалетната?" - Sister, where is the toilet? - She asks me. "Ела." - Come. - I answer and walk her towards the washroom. "Джонатан, или там какъвто беше, гадже ли ти е?"- Jonathan, or whatever his name is, is he your boyfriend? - I laugh and open the door to the washroom. "Ами, май така стана..." - Well, it seems so...

"От кога?" - Since when? - she asks entering the toilet. "Днес." - Today. - Viktoria opens back the door after a while and we go back to the livingroom. "I think I get what you were talking about..." Jonathan says while coming towards me. "What happened?" I ask looking around. "Your mother and father..." I stop him. "I get it!" *That means that they had a "fight" again*. "They are like 5-years-olds," I say with a smile on my face. "Како, хайде спаринг." - Sister, let's do a sparring match. - My brother, Peter, says coming to me. "You do sparring matches?!" Jonathan says looking at both of us. I understand him. Peter is almost 30 centimeters higher than me and he is huge. And here is me, 161cm, 48 kilograms. It seems logical that just after seconds sparring with my brother, I will be smacked on the wall looking as if I was fighting with a tornado. "We do," I answer Jonathan. "Let's do it."

We are in my training room and I and my brother are warming up. Everyone is sitting or standing and looking at us as if we are going to beat each other up for real and it's not just a sparring match. We take our positions and I see Taehyung's smirk. My brother takes the first step and tries to attack but I catch his arm, place my right foot on his hip, then my left one while the right goes around his neck and with the weight of my body I spin and put him on the ground. Jonathan's eyes grew bigger. My mother places her hand on her mouth, my father is motionless and with no exact facial expression. Viktoria laughs and Taehyung's smirk is now bigger. My bother stands up. "Are you okay?" I ask him. He nods and attacks again. I fall down with a split, grab his leg and pull it towards me, so he falls on his back. I smile. "Don't be this much easy on me," I tease him. "Okay."

I am about to punch him but he ditches my fist, grabs my hands, and turns me around so my back faces his chest. "Like this?" I smile. "Better," I twist my hands, lay on my back between Peter's legs, and with a kick on his ass, I push myself away from him while he losses his balance for a while. I get up quickly. "But not enough." I grab two wooden sticks and give him one of them. "Let's see what you can do with this." I lower my center with the stick in my left hand behind my back, my right hand in front of me in a resting fist.

Chapter 18

"I still can't believe how you did all that. You move so quickly! And the moment you broke his stick with a kick! That was amazing!" I laugh while listening to Jonathan being in awe. "I think, we should do a sparring match, too." I put my fork down and look at everyone on the dining table. "Maybe," I answer him and grab my glass of water. Out of nowhere, the picture of me and him sparring came in my mind and I choke on the water. Jonathan smirks. "We can do that there, too." He whispers and I look at him with my eyes wide still choking. "Are you, by any chance, a mind-reader?" I ask him with a final cough in the end. "It's written on your face, baby." He answers whispering close to my ear and I feel his breath on my skin. "I doubt that," I grab my fork again. "I am popular with my blank facial expression. You are just... a mind-reader." I smile.

"I am sure everyone, who sees a blank expression on your face, hasn't slept with you and probably doesn't know and understand you." He says and takes a bite of his potatoes with chicken and vegan mayonnaise. I look at him once again. Then, I look away. "I value your point of view, and I appreciate your kind words, but I don't think you know me either." Jonathan places his hand on my shoulder. "I didn't say I know you. Or that I understand you completely. But I am sure I do much more to understand you than the other people on this table. About knowing you, Taehyung beats me with 100 points. But that's just for now." He winks. "Извинете ме! Excuse me!" I say bowing and stand up. I head outside. "What did you do?" Taehyung asks and I hear him standing up, too. I close the door behind me. Right after, it's open again by Taehyung. "Hey, what's up?"

"He wants to get to know me," I answer Taehyung his unasked question. "That was likely to happen. You know that. He's your boyfriend now!" I clench my jaw. "I know. But I can't let this happen. He knows way too much right now. What about the next week? Month? I know this is not the right way to deal with psychological trauma and problems in my life but I have to tell him I need time. And if I have to tell him another story, I will." Silence fills in the atmosphere for a while. Taehyung places a hand on my shoulder. "Okay. When are you gonna do this?" I turn around to face him. "The sooner, the better," I say and open the door. "Let's go inside." When we get close to the table, Taehyung sits down. I go up to mom and tell her that I will be upstairs because I've got a headache. I close and lock the door.

"Karolina!" I hear from the other side of the door. "Mind unlocking the door?" Jonathan asks. I just stay silent hoping he will just give up and go away. "Come on. You can't just lock your boyfriend out of the bedroom." I frown and feel my blood rushing through my veins. My heart racing up. I get up with fury, unlock, and open the door. The moment I see Jonathan, I grab him by the hand and get him in. I lock the door again. "Boyfriend?!" I say angrily trying to hold myself up. "So the things you did... coming in my life and fuck me, then coming in my personal space with the phrase 'You don't just sleep with anyone, right' and then trying to get to the core of my being in just a few days... is this a real relationship for you, Jonathan? Because for me, it's at least months friendship, so we have time to get to actually know each other and then it comes to the next stage and the next one! I am sorry, Jonathan. I realize you were heartbroken and I understand your pain but... all this, it's not right." Jonathan just keeps looking at me.

"It is probably for the best if we are just friends for now. And I really think it was for the best that your father didn't come..." I say and unlock the door. "Karolina, what exactly is the reason you are breaking up with me?" He asks me looking into my eyes. "I better know the real reason. And not the angry version." I nod. "I am sorry, but the angry version is true. We know each other for less than a week. And I am just not ready." He frowns and comes closer to me. "Why? What happened?" I shake my head while trying to hold my tears. "All that... you... it's overwhelming. You want to know about me so much more than it's even allowed. More than I would allow. And if you really get to know some aspects of my personality, you will really be disappointed." He looks at me with confusion in his eyes. "Tell me."

"Jonathan..." He places his hands on my shoulders. "Tell me!" I bite my lips. "I am just the kind of person that can not stay in a relationship. I like my independence. My freedom. I enjoy being alone. Doing things on my own. I love risking... and sometimes I take unnecessary risks about my life. And you are so warm-hearted and ready... I just can not..." And his lips are on mine. I push him away before giving in completely. "No, Jonathan!" I almost shout when he starts to get closer again. "No!" I slap him. "Don't get any closer! I told you enough! Now get out of my house and spend Christmas with your relatives!" He looks at me. "I may leave now. But I'm not giving up on you!"

Chapter 19

It's Christmas Day and I am supposed to at least smile more, but the story with Jonathan is still in my head, and the only one responsible for it is me. Nevertheless, my family's presence is what I am grateful for right now. Taehyung had to finally go back to his team members. Erica had to return to her girlfriend. So now, I am unpacking presents with my family around the Christmas tree. My phone starts ringing. "Ей сега се връщам..." - I'll be right back... - I say and go to the kitchen. "Frederick?!" I say picking up the phone. "Merry Christmas, Karolina. Sorry for calling you at this time and on this day but I need you." Frederick, a general of the army in Russia, says making a little worried. *If he calls me, that means some important stuff is going on. Otherwise, he has other people to do the work.*

"What is it?" I ask getting right to the point. "Dr. Wilson disappeared during a mission in Alaska. Along with the whole team there. There are no traces, no clues, nothing. It's like they have never been there!" I open my laptop and open the files about the mission. "When did they disappear?" I ask when I see the mission should have finished a month ago. "A week ago," Frederick answers me. "What do you have so far?" I look at the details about the mission, the goal... "I already told you. Nothing! The last message was that they need more time because of the weather." I raise my left eyebrow, put my right hand on my chin, and look at the laptop's screen. "You can not find anything if the weather was like what it is written here. The traces... everything must be erased because of the snowstorm. Do you have the paperwork on their work?" I cross my legs. "We do..." He answers hesitantly. "Send them to me!" I tell him and close the files. "I might have an idea of how to find them." I smile, put the laptop aside, and stand up. "Thank you, Karolina."

"You are more than welcome!" I hang up. "От работа ли ти звъняха?" - Work-related call? - I nod in answer to my mother. "Това е да си шеф." - This is what it's like to be a boss. - I say teasingly. "Стана късно и съм уморена, затова отивам в стаята си." - It's late and I'm tired, so I'm going to my room. - I say with a made smile on, grab my laptop, and rush to the stairs. I lock the door and sit on my bed with the laptop on my nightstand and my legs crossed. I see Frederick, aka Ivan, has sent me the files with paperwork. I pick my phone up. "Zack, hello. I need you to rearrange my flight to tomorrow morning at 8. Can you do that for me?"

"Of course, Kar! Why so fast?" He asks a little breathy. "Rick called. He said he has some work for me and you know, I can not work without my gadgets." Something in the background murmurs. "So it's something big!?" I smirk. "It is. By the way, the flight is for me and my family. So get Sam acknowledged." Sam is my privet pilot and usually, when I need a fast, reliable pilot, he is the person. "What's so important, Fedorova?" And we just got serious. "Work, Cortney! Just important work that needs to be done as soon as possible. Frederick counts on me for it!" Zack humphs.

"Okay. Stay safe." I nod. "I will. Thank you!" *Now I have to disappoint my dad.*

Chapter 20

Yesterday after I called my biological father and told him that because of super important business, that literally is based on life or death, I will be busy and will not be able to enjoy The New Year with them, I packed my luggage for the morning and told my family to do the same because they are not going to have time to do so in the morning. And because of the rush I put them in, I had to explain to them the same story I told my biological father. The story was simple and partly true - that some employees in my company were sent in Alaska for an investigation, and no one ever heard of them for a week.

They believed me, which I am grateful for, and now here we are, in the middle of a road about to get in my own airplane. "Zack! Hello! I thought you were staying with your family for the holidays!" I say, hugging him. "Oh, and Zack, this is my family! Това е Зак Кърни, моят главен асистент!" - This is Zack Corney, my main assistant! - They all nod, and I do them a sign to take their seats. As I take mine, I open the laptop and take out my homemade snack, pistachios with almond flour, and salt. My favorite! I open the files of some deals I have to make after I go back to Honolulu, but then I hear a familiar voice. "I see Zack kept his promise of not informing you about me and my little visit." I lift my head up, and I can't believe it! "Alyson! What are you doing here?"

"I can't believe you just said that! I came here to see you!" She hugs me. "Now, this is for you!" She gives me a box, not a very small one. I look at it with confusion. "I know you don't like presents, but I am here to shake you up a little bit." I smile and start ripping the paper of the box. "You know, someone already shook my life up pretty well, but I guess it is never enough, and a little more will be just fine." I open it and see a book, a watch, and a magazine. I lift my eyes up to look at her. "Because I know you love learning, and you value your time. And the magazine is for you to move your hormones a little bit." I lift my eyebrow up and take the magazine. "What do you mean?" I ask and see the main points in it. 'Most sexy men', 'Most desired and successful men'...

"Are you kidding me?" I throw at her a glare while opening the magazine. I never liked such things, and she knows it. A familiar face pops up, and I return to the previous page. "Jonathan?!" I say, looking at his face on the page under number 2 on a category 'Most desired and successful men' "You really must be kidding me!" I say, still looking at him. "You know him?" Alyson asks me. "Yeah..." I close the magazine and put it aside. "Nevermind!" I grab the book. "Oh, do you really think I am going to leave it like this? You, obviously, know one of the hottest men in our world, and you expect me not to ask questions?"

"I have read this book." I say shaking 'Birthright' By Nora Roberts in my hand. "Long time ago. But it's one of my favorites, so thanks." I put the book over the magazine and see Alyson shaking her head. "Okay, but I am not telling you everything," I say because I know her and her ability to goo on my nerves, especially when it comes to romance. "We were together for a while. It was not anything serious." She puts her hand over her mouth. "You slept with him?! You had sex with Jonathan Edmeades?!" I shake my head. *I will be sorry about that!* "We did. But again, nothing serious."

"Nonsense! He is not that kind of a man. He is very warm-hearted and is known for his-" I interrupt her. "Stubbornness!" She shakes her head and hands. "I don't know about that, but he is really devoted to his relationships. At least, the last ones. He was the biggest playboy before that." I open my mouth and close it a few times. "Really?" I menage to ask. "Oh, yeah. It looks like you don't know much about him. It is not in your style." I nod. "You are right. It isn't." *And it definitely was not in my style to have sex with a stranger, but I guess everyone has his or her moments*. My phone lights up and starts ringing. I see Jonathan's name on the screen. "We are talking about the sexiest man, and he is calling me." I pick up seeing Alyson's focus is now just and only on me. "What?" I ask, with my voice a little harsher than I thought it would be. "Why are you so angry?" He prompts instead of answering my question. "Jonathan, tell me why you are calling, or I am hanging up! I am busy!"

"I am calling you to invite you to celebrate The New Year with me." I look at Alyson, who is nodding like crazy. "No!" I respond. "I am not asking you to come to my bedroom naked, even though I don't deny I would love to taste your body again." I grab my head with one hand when I see

Alyson's read face while trying not to scream and, or laugh. I show her my middle finger. "And it's not going to be just us. There are going to have lots of people."

"I am not saying no because I don't want to celebrate. I am replying to you this way because I will be tied up!" I explain myself to him. "Can't you free yourself of your occupations for an hour?"I take a deep breath. "I can't. I am even flying to Bulgaria to leave my family with a wish for The New Year, and then I am heading to Seattle." Alyson looks at me questionably. "We will talk later about that." I lift my eyebrows. "As soon as I remember, we broke the short affair we had." I close my eyes. This sentence sounded way too rude. I am not turning my old habits into action. "I am sorry! Sometimes I am mean without meaning to."

"We will talk later, Karolina." He hangs up. "How could you say all that?" Alyson shouts. I roll my eyes. "I told him the truth!" I defend myself and relax into my seat. His words come back in my mind. 'I am not asking you to come to my bedroom naked, even though I don't deny I would love to taste your body again.' My body reacts by sending a sweet vibration down to my sensitive part. I bite my bottom lip. My breath quickens. It can't be! How is it even possible to turn me on with just words? "Are you listening to me?" Alyson scolds me. "Sorry, I had my head in the clouds." She smirks. "Clouds or a cloud named Jonathan?"I look at her as deadly as I can in this situation. "Okay, I am sorry! I am becoming serious!" She moves so that her body faces mine. "What is going on between you two? And how the hell did you end up with him?" She starts asking questions. I explained to her the story without many details. I told her about the meeting in the forest, then in the grocery store, and the date that, actually, did not happen because of the snowstorm. After that, I informed her briefly about the passionate nights and fights we had. And, in the end, I described her the last heated conversation we experienced. "All this is crazy! For your information! And, by the way, the boy is head over heels in love with you."

"Thank you for letting me know." I sarcastically noted, and I cross my arms. "I want to point out that he is not only looking like a sex god but also sounds like one." I laugh. "According to your words and your expressions, while even thinking about him, he really is a sex god." I close my eyes for some seconds.* I enjoyed him over me, inside of me, next to me... Oh, Jesus!* "Can we change the theme of the conversation?" She laughs and nods. *I have to distract myself and keep working. Work! That is it!* "Actually, I have a lot of work! Let's talk later!"

Chapter 21

"Okay," Jonathan whispers and hugs me tightly, my head resting on his chest. I grab a blanket from the couch across us and cover our bodies with it. "I am a very ambitious and independent person, and I have been one since I remember myself. Regardless of my age, I have always believed, I can go through everything life throws at me. And since I have always wanted to change a lot of things in the world, I planned and did everything I could to get up to here, where I am right now. And I still am working on realizing some of my plans." I take a shaky deep breath when I notice my body starts shaking a bit. "I am whole-heartedly devoted to my goals, and I have no problem being by myself. I love my space! And after I had my heart broken a few times, the last one being the most severe case, I decided that I still can give and receive love even if I am not in a relationship. And the fact that I don't mind being alone and am capable of someday adopting a child I can raise made the decision even easier." I adjust myself, so I can face Jonathan directly and look at his beautiful warm deep brown eyes.

"What I mean by all that is... I am an entrepreneur and in the middle of a deal with a fashion company. I am a writer! I am the CEO of many companies. HTSolutions or High Tech Solutions, BeLifeUp, WSA - World Science Administration, and HTFR. The last one stands for..." I pause, biting my lips. "High Tech Fighting Robots." His look changes, now becoming more curious and awaiting. "It is a company selling robots for purposes like teaching humans how to protect themselves better without anyone getting hurt, which is what most people know about the company..."

Jonathan looks at me a little confused. "I still don't get where you are going with all that." He says, looking straight into my eyes. One of the other purposes is for the armies' uses. But sometimes, I not only provide help to these counties by selling them robots. Sometimes, I risk my own life. I am not telling him that part of the story. "Well, all the things take most of my time. A lot of times, it is from 9 in the morning to late nights. I go around the world, and you said you do, too. Even if we get together and all that stuff, we will barely have time for each other. You know, forget that! We can handle it." I stand up as I sense feelings in me starts building up.

"The problem, even though it may seem like a cliche, is in me! I am afraid of getting this much close to someone! I thought I overcame it, but it is now obvious that I didn't! I am terrified of sharing my whole life with someone because I don't want to depend on anyone! I don't want someone telling me what to do! I love my freedom! I love my space! I love being a leader!" I inhale slowly, feeling my eyes are filling up with tears. "And the fact, I love you being with me, by my side, on the top of me, inside of me..." I sit on the sofa again, looking straight into his carefully watching me soft eyes. "And then, when I hear, see, sense or think of you, I want to cuddle into you and spend as much time as I can with you!" I weep my tears off and clear my throat. Taking a shaky deep breath, I continue.

"I know I should work on these issues. I am working on them. But I can't live with you and hide things from you!" Jonathan frowns. Taking my hands in his, making it clear he is and will be here for me, even if my actions and words start making no sense at all. "I don't know what more is inside your precious head, but I want you to remind yourself of my last words in that cabin!" I shake my head. "Jonathan, you don't understand!" He squeezes my hands coming a little closer to me. "Then explain it to me! I will try and understand you! I will always do that! And about what you said earlier..." He pauses for a few seconds, searching for the right words. "I will never even think about controlling you! And I doubt you can actually depend on something or someone."

"Jonathan..." I look away and move my hands away from his. "I appreciate it all, but you can't do this!" He comes closer to me, entering aggressively into my space. "Why?" He insists, his voice calm but at the same time with a note of pain. He places his hand on my cheek, making me look at him. "Because if you do, your life will be a hell!" I answer as coldly as I can. "No! What the fuck! What do you mean?" He asks, now truly confused. "I do things most of them, which I can not even mention! Things that risk my life!" I say as I grab my clothes from the ground. Well, the unripped ones of them. "You are making me worried!" He stands up after me and puts on his boxer. "You don't need to worry about me! I can take of myself! I have been doing so far, and I can keep doing it!"

While still collecting my clothes from the floor, I walk to my bedroom with Jonathan after me. "You said most of which you can't mention. Tell me the ones you can talk about!" He persists as I open the door. From there, I enter in my closet to grab something to wear. "Jonathan, I am not talking about that!" I choose an oversized black T-shirt and leggings in the same color. "Are you kidding me? First, you mention something knowing, I will want to know more! Then you say you are NOT talking about it!" He shouts now. Great! Just great! I turn to face him as we are both finally with clothes on. "I know! I am sorry! I can't make my own mind up! And now I confused you, too!" With determination radiating from his whole being, he gets closer to me and pins me against the wall.

Jonathan looks at me carefully. "You are making me go crazy!" He smashes his lips on mine. I moan unwillingly, and he uses this opportunity to enter his tongue in my mouth. My hormones fire up. "Jonathan, we shouldn't-" He places his finger on my lips. "I don't know what's so troublesome. And maybe I will not understand it soon. But I will be by your side, and when you are ready, I will be there and listen to you. No judgemental! Now, give in the moment and spend the rest of the night in my embrace. We can talk, watch a movie, dance, eat, whatever you want." The whole time his eyes were on mine. This small gesture of pure love makes my eyes tear up. "You are so stubborn!" I laugh a little. "Let's give in!" I say and intertwine our hands.

Chapter 22

"Okay," Jonathan whispers and hugs me tightly, my head resting on his chest. I grab a blanket from the couch across us and cover our bodies with it. "I am a very ambitious and independent person, and I have been one since I remember myself. Regardless of my age, I have always believed, I can go through everything life throws at me. And since I have always wanted to change a lot of things in the world, I planned and did everything I could to get up to here, where I am right now. And I still am working on realizing some of my plans." I take a shaky deep breath when I notice my body starts shaking a bit. "I am whole-heartedly devoted to my goals, and I have no problem being by myself. I love my space! And after I had my heart broken a few times, the last one being the most severe case, I decided that I still can give and receive love even if I am not in a relationship. And the fact that I don't mind being alone and am capable of someday adopting a child I can raise made the decision even easier." I adjust myself, so I can face Jonathan directly and look at his beautiful warm deep brown eyes.

"What I mean by all that is... I am an entrepreneur and in the middle of a deal with a fashion company. I am a writer! I am the CEO of many companies. HTSolutions or High Tech Solutions, BeLifeUp, WSA - World Science Administration, and HTFR. The last one stands for..." I pause, biting my lips. "High Tech Fighting Robots." His look changes, now becoming more curious and awaiting. "It is a company selling robots for purposes like teaching humans how to protect themselves better without anyone getting hurt, which is what most people know about the company..."

Jonathan looks at me a little confused. "I still don't get where you are going with all that." He says, looking straight into my eyes. One of the other purposes is for the armies' uses. But sometimes, I not only provide help to these counties by selling them robots. Sometimes, I risk my own life. I am not telling him that part of the story. "Well, all the things take most of my time. A lot of times, it is from 9 in the morning to late nights. I go around the world, and you said you do, too. Even if we get together and all that stuff, we will barely have time for each other. You know, forget that! We can handle it." I stand up as I sense feelings in me starts building up.

"The problem, even though it may seem like a cliche, is in me! I am afraid of getting this much close to someone! I thought I overcame it, but it is now obvious that I didn't! I am terrified of sharing my whole life with someone because I don't want to depend on anyone! I don't want someone telling me what to do! I love my freedom! I love my space! I love being a leader!" I inhale slowly, feeling my eyes are filling up with tears. "And the fact, I love you being with me, by my side, on the top of me, inside of me..." I sit on the sofa again, looking straight into his carefully watching me soft eyes. "And then, when I hear, see, sense or think of you, I want to cuddle into you and spend as much time as I can with you!" I weep my tears off and clear my throat. Taking a shaky deep breath, I continue.

"I know I should work on these issues. I am working on them. But I can't live with you and hide things from you!" Jonathan frowns. Taking my hands in his, making it clear he is and will be here for me, even if my actions and words start making no sense at all. "I don't know what more is inside your precious head, but I want you to remind yourself of my last words in that cabin!" I shake my head. "Jonathan, you don't understand!" He squeezes my hands coming a little closer to me. "Then explain it to me! I will try and understand you! I will always do that! And about what you said earlier..." He pauses for a few seconds, searching for the right words. "I will never even think about controlling you! And I doubt you can actually depend on something or someone."

"Jonathan..." I look away and move my hands away from his. "I appreciate it all, but you can't do this!" He comes closer to me, entering aggressively into my space. "Why?" He insists, his voice calm but at the same time with a note of pain. He places his hand on my cheek, making me look at him. "Because if you do, your life will be a hell!" I answer as coldly as I can. "No! What the fuck! What do you mean?" He asks, now truly confused. "I do things most of them, which I can not even mention! Things that risk my life!" I say as I grab my clothes from the ground. Well, the unripped ones of them. "You are making me worried!" He stands up after me and puts on his boxer. "You don't need to worry about me! I can take of myself! I have been doing so far, and I can keep doing it!"

While still collecting my clothes from the floor, I walk to my bedroom with Jonathan after me. "You said most of which you can't mention. Tell me the ones you can talk about!" He persists as I open the door. From there, I enter in my closet to grab something to wear. "Jonathan, I am not talking about that!" I choose an oversized black T-shirt and leggings in the same color. "Are you kidding me? First, you mention something knowing, I will want to know more! Then you say you are NOT talking about it!" He shouts now. Great! Just great! I turn to face him as we are both finally with clothes on. "I know! I am sorry! I can't make my own mind up! And now I confused you, too!" With determination radiating from his whole being, he gets closer to me and pins me against the wall.

Jonathan looks at me carefully. "You are making me go crazy!" He smashes his lips on mine. I moan unwillingly, and he uses this opportunity to enter his tongue in my mouth. My hormones fire up. "Jonathan, we shouldn't-" He places his finger on my lips. "I don't know what's so troublesome. And maybe I will not understand it soon. But I will be by your side, and when you are ready, I will be there and listen to you. No judgemental! Now, give in the moment and spend the rest of the night in my embrace. We can talk, watch a movie, dance, eat, whatever you want." The whole time his eyes were on mine. This small gesture of pure love makes my eyes tear up. "You are so stubborn!" I laugh a little. "Let's give in!" I say and intertwine our hands.

Chapter 23

I wake up in my soft bed and look around. My watch says it is 4:03 AM, and the still not risen sun confirms it. However, the pearl-white walls make the room brighter. I look through the wall-length windows and enjoy the view of the sleeping city while waiting for my morning heart rate check-up. It shows 65 beats per minute. Perfect! I get up, putting a long over-sized T-shirt, and head outside of the bedroom in search of Jonathan. Maybe he left, my mind tells me. But when I enter the living room seeing a man looking through the window deep in thoughts, I understand that my mind or most likely, a self-destroying belief was wrong. He is here. "Hey, have you slept?" I ask, getting closet to him and hugging him from behind.

He nods, grabbing my hands and squeezing them. I let go of his grip and go in front of him so I can face him. "Look, I know I have been harsh..." He interrupts me with a kiss. "Darling, please, let's not starts the upcoming day like this." I nod, looking at his face, letting myself remember every curve of his beautiful face. "But we will have to discuss what we are going to do later." He smiles. "I know. You don't leave work unfinished." Jonathan kisses my forehead. "Neither do I. So be sure about talking about it later."

"Do you know how we can spice up our morning?" I ask while scrambling eggs in a big bowl, Jonathan shrugs his shoulders while slicing a green pepper. We are now in the kitchen preparing breakfast after completing a productive morning routine. I shake my head a little and look at my watch. It shows 7 AM. The walls are soundproof, which means 'Go, girl!'. "Ana, turn on AJ playlist." The music, and more specifically, Alan Jackson's Country Boy, starts playing, and I let myself move with the rhythm. "Are you kidding me?!" Jonathan's voice gets me out of my trance. "What?" I ask wondering what just happened. "You listen to Alan Jackson?!" I nod. "Uncle Paul is going to like you!" I smile. "Uncle Paul?"

"My dad's brother. He is a big fan of country music..." He leaves the knife on the kitchen plot. "And the lifestyle, too. Probably because we are from Tennessee, Bristol. But that's another thing. He loves Alan Jackson!" I sit on a chair and leave the bowl with the eggs in it aside. "Tell me more!" I say, almost commanding, showing my curious nature. "Well, our roots start in Bristol. And, my family never actually got out of there. My father was the first one to leave the traditions aside by deciding he wants, you know, to be a successful businessman. As for me, I love both. Most of the time, I am a businessman like my father. I can not leave my people. And I love what I do so, yeah. But whenever I want to, I am more than welcome to my family's ranch."

"That's amazing!" I say with awe. I always had a thing for Tennessee, and country lifestyle. "Actually, I plan on visiting my uncle right after The New Year celebration. And I would love it if you come with me." I open my mouth and close it. I bite my lip. "I would love to. But it all depends on what a turn the whole thing between us is going to take. We don't know what will happen. But, if everything is okay, count me in." Jonathan kisses me, and then 'Good Time' is what I hear. "I love this song!" I say, dancing and taking a pan for the eggs.

Jonathan laughs when I pretend to play on a guitar. "It's time for a good time!" I sing, moving around with my invisible guitar. "A shot of tequila." Jonathan starts singing, and I look at him with an open mouth. I slap him on the shoulder. "Why didn't you tell me earlier you know the song?" I say with a smile on my face. "I thought it's obvious. I am from Tennessee." I shake my head. 'Little Bitty' is the next song, and I hear Jonathan singing to me, "And a little bitty girl." instead of 'a little bitty car.' and I slap him once again. "Well, it's alright to be little bitty," he goes on, and I laugh. I put coconut oil in the pan, and I grab the bowl with sliced peppers and put them in it. And while doing so, I hear Jonathan yelling, "Yeeeaaahhhh!" along with Alan Jackson.

I burst out laughing while taking care of the peppers, so they don't burn. I look at Jonathan, who is now dancing and coming closer to me. "Might as well share, might as well smile," he sings and sticks his tongue out. "What has gotten into you?" I ask, laughing. "Tennessee, girl!" He grabs me and spins me around. "I see!" I say when he places me back on the ground. "Why don't you spend New Year there then?" I curiously ask. "No way! I am staying with you!" Jonathan kisses me. "Who says I will not be with you?" His eyes grow big, and a beautiful wide smile appears on his face. True happiness is on his face. I love seeing him this way. "Are you serious?" I nod.

"I will make a few phone calls, and I will work a little bit more in the next few days. And it's done." I go to the pan

to mix the peppers with the eggs. "It should do the work."
I turn to face him. "Thank you!" He kisses my forehead. I
smile. "Let's eat breakfast now."

Chapter 24

"Hey, Rick. I will be able to help only with the information." I say before him saying something else. After I thought about it with all the details, think meetings, personal work, and business, I could only think about helping from a distance. And keep in mind that I am halfway done. "I know, Kar. Don't worry! That would be more than enough! I know you are a busy woman with lots of responsibilities. And you have a personal life, too. So, thank you for doing even that." I smile. He has always been this way. Thankful, positive, and cheerful.

"Okay. Listen now, then! I want a team searching under the snow. In the last few days, the snowstorm was a disaster! Let them dive deep. We don't want to miss anything! One more thing of importance is to look at the Satelite recordings. I know it may be hard, torturing, and slow to do so because the information we need is on a more secret level, but this may save lives. Try to get there. That's it for now. Call me when you have something for me." I get in my royal blue Porsche Taycan and wait for Zack's answer. "Okay. All clear!" I hang up and take the turn to get out of the underground parking lot.

The humidity is high, 98%, and the air feels a lot colder than it is. The streets are wet, most of the city is covered in beautiful white snow, and the chance of accidents occurring is pretty high if you are not prepared. But, since we are in Seattle where the bad weather is something that happens often, and with it now being winter, accidents because of such a reason are less common. The sky is still covered with dark clouds, making the sunrise less visible. The traffic is non-existent because most people are now waking up, at 7:30 AM, so I am enjoying the ride while Alan Walker's 'Faded' is playing in the background singing.

My fingers are moving gently on the wheel while enjoying the view and driving. Jonathan is at my apartment, preparing his luggage as tonight we are leaving for Tennesse, Bristol. I take a left turn and listen as Two Feet's 'Go Fuck Yourself' starts playing. My mind directly goes to the night I and Jonathan shared. As every single one of the other nights, this one is special, filled with emotions, and touching. We talked a lot.

I managed to explain to him that, whatever I am doing, it will not have an impact on our relationships. Then he came up with the fact that if there is one lie, there will be more. He was right. And knowing that damn well, I told him the truth - that even if I want to explain to him everything, I couldn't do it, simply because there are people who are ruling and I am not one of them. He, of course, understood me and said that if it doesn't depend on me, he wouldn't push me. But it does, a little, but it does. And so, determined, I called for a meeting with *the boss*.

I stop in front of two other black Mercedes Benz Suv automobiles with dark window tint in the middle of a parking lot. "Г-н иванович!" - Mr. Ivanovich! - I greet him politely as a huge, built man with blue eyes and dirty blonde hair gets out of the car escorted by a few bodyguards. "Госпожа Федорова, о чем весь этот шум?" - Mrs. Fedorova, what's all the fuss about? - he asks me right away as he gets closer. "Я сожалею об этом. Я должен поговорить с вами о проблеме, которая возникла в результате работы на вас." - I am sorry about it. I have to talk to you about the problem that was created by working for you.

"Я слушаю." - I am listening. - he says seriously, looking right into my eyes. "Мне приятно работать с вами, но человек, с которым я пытаюсь установить связь на более глубоком уровне, задает вопросы, поскольку я сказал ему, что не могу быть с ним и лгать ему." - Working for you is a pleasure for me but a person who I am trying to connect with on a deeper level is asking questions since I told him I can not be with him and lie to him. - I start carefully choosing my words. "Вариантов немного. Либо я скажу ему, что работаю с тобой. Или я больше не помогаю. Я не могу с кем-то и врать. Особенно когда это означает, что когда-нибудь я не вернусь." - The options are not many. It's either I tell him I work with you. Or I am not helping anymore. I can not with someone and lie. Especially when it means that someday I may not come back.

"Я понимаю. Но вы не можете сказать ему, что работаете с российской армией. Если у вас есть

разрешение от американцев, это их собственный риск."
- I understand. But you can't tell him you work with the Russian army. If you have a permission from the Americans, it's their own risk. - he says, his voice direct and bossy. "Я не прошу вас говорить ему именно это. Прошу сказать ему следующее. Все, что я делаю, - это помогаю организациям в выполнении их миссий. Это правда. Я просто не говорю, что это за организации." - I am not asking you to tell him exactly that. I am asking you to tell him the following. That all that I do is helping organizations with their missions. It is the truth. I am just not mentioning what the organizations are. - he looks at me with joy in his skyblue eyes.

"Вы умны, Федорова." - You are smart, Fedorova. - he pauses and looks at the view. The white snow, the tall buildings pointing at the sky. "Ладно. Вы можете рассказать своему особому человеку свою версию правды." - Okay. You can tell your special person your version of the truth. - he says at the end with a bright smile that makes me smile, too. "Хорошего дня, Федорова. И счастливых праздников!" - Have a great day, Fedorova. And happy holidays! - I nod, and we both get in our cars. *Jonathan, here I come with news.*

Chapter 25

"Is that it?" Jonathan asks me, his right eyebrow up. "It is. I just needed permission because the organizations I work with are privet. And even though all that I do is helping them with their missions, sometimes it includes fighting and guns." I explain as if it all was a game and grab my phone. "What do you mean by fighting and guns?" I face him and see the worry in his eyes that are also telling me he is impatient for answers. "Well, fighting and guns. Sometimes people don't want something to happen, so they kidnap, murder, or hurt the people that want that thing to happen or to be found. And my job is to find artifacts, find the kidnapped, or sometimes, by protecting myself, even kill." I look at his eyes, waiting for a reaction. "So, that's why you said you risk your life..." I nod m head in an answer.

"Why are you doing it?" He asks me somehow lost in thoughts. I swallow hard. "Because I crave adventure, and it gives even more sense of a purpose. I know it seems crazy craving such kind of experiences, but I've always loved playing with weapons and fighting while completing a mission. When I was a little girl and then a teenager, I used to go to the forest to climb, jump, and hide. I practiced fighting in all the possible places, and wherever I was, I thought of the fastest, most efficient way to escape and what I could use as a weapon." I pause, realizing how crazy all of it sounds. "I will understand if you want to leave," I add in the end and wait for his response. Jonathan looks me in the eyes, confused. "Why would I want such a thing?"

"Well, some people don't want to mess with someone who endangers their lives," I answer and shrug. He comes closer to me on the sofa and grabs my hands. "Well," he starts, "I am falling in love with you. This means, no matter what you do, I am going to be by your side." I nod and hug him. "Thank you. But do you realize what you are involving in?" I ask him. "I do. Otherwise, I wouldn't be here, still listening to you."

"That makes sense!" I respond and pull away from the hug. "Now... I wanted to do something if everything turns out to be alright as it happened to be." I smile a little and kiss him, giving him a hint of what's to come.

Second Book

Expect book 2, "Nights Like This", of "Naughty Nights" series soon. I am sending you all the love and light! Take care and be ready for the new ride!